Too Close for Comfort

Too Close for Comfort

La Jill Hunt

www.urbanbooks.net

Urban Books, LLC
97 N18th Street
Wyandanch, NY 11798

ISBN 13: 978-1-60162-685-1
ISBN 10: 1-60162-685-1

First Mass Market Printing March 2015
First Trade Paperback Printing November 2006
Printed in the United States of America

10 9 8 7 6 5 4 3 2 1

This is a work of fiction. Any references or similarities to actual events, real people, living, or dead, or to real locales are intended to give the novel a sense of reality. Any similarity in other names, characters, places, and incidents is entirely coincidental.

Distributed by Kensington Publishing Corp.
Submit Orders to:
Customer Service
400 Hahn Road
Westminster, MD 21157-4627
Phone: 1-800-733-3000
Fax: 1-800-659-2436

Acknowledgments

Father, God, in Heaven, You know I always have to thank You first. For the insight, the talent, the opportunity and the strength to do this once again. Your grace and mercy have once again brought me through and I'm living this moment because of You.

To my parents, my grandmother and especially to my daughters, for having the strength to endure. It wasn't easy, but it was worth it . . . I love you.

To my beloved Pastor Kim W. Brown, for all of your leadership and brutal honesty as I continue on this journey and walk in my favor. To Elder Valerie K. Brown, for all of your constant encouragement and advice and most of all for challenging me to just do it! I will never, ever, ever forget those words . . . in the true essence of Oprah, that was my "ah ha" moment and I love you for it! To my Mt. Lebanon Missionary Baptist Church Family, your prayers, smiles and support are to be commended. I couldn't ask for a better support system.

To my brother/cousin Braxton, the older we get, the closer we become and I thank God that we are able to share our accomplishments together. I always have your back . . . and now that book four has dropped, maybe one day I will pay my cell phone bill on time, LOL.

To my girls, Joy, Shan, Saundra, Tonya, Cherie, Robin, Mechellene, Pam, Toye, Roxanne and Selena . . . no matter the reason, or the season . . . you are my lifetime friends.

To my guys, Roy Glenn, Dwayne S. Joseph, K Elliott, Big CTY, Chris Booker and Torrance Oxendine . . . you always got my back and I love you for it.

To Carl Weber, although I piss you off, I know you still love me and I'll always be your li'l sister . . . one day I'm gonna make you proud, just wait and see. To Martha Weber, who causes me to inhale every time I sit down to write . . . you are so special and I thank you for leading me in my craft.

To Yvette Lewis, you know you are the best friend/personal assistant/business partner/personal shopper/stylist/therapist/beauty consultant/loan officer a girl could have . . . love ya!!!

Acknowledgments

I gotta thank 'DA ROW' at work for putting up with the chit chatter as I talked about what I was gonna write about: Angela Burleigh, Donna Gwathney, Jodina Ford, Chenay Cuffee, Ms. Susan Allgood, Andrea Jones, and Dawn James . . . y'all have got to be the most hilarious people in the world.

To Omedia Cutler, Milly Avent, and Crystal "Nardsbaby' Gamble . . . you are THE BOMB! I couldn't ask for a better reading crew!

To David L. Porter, my rainbow at the end of the storm . . . for yelling and pushing and ignoring me for days; not accepting my attempts at procrastination . . . thanks for reminding me this isn't even about me and who it's for . . . I love you!!!

To Kym Lee, the baddest makeup artist the world has ever seen. Thank you for your time and talent and sharing your stories with me . . . if they think Yaya is wild in this book, wait until the real deal hits stores. You are a true gift and I am blessed to even know you.

To the other folks, who are always in my corner: Arvita, Robilyn, Ms. Frankie, Cheryl, Danita, Yolanda, Vicki, and Tasha . . . thank you.

To Stephanie Wilkerson and LaTonya Townes who stepped up at the last minute, literally and helped me pull it together! You are no joke and I appreciate you!

Acknowledgments

To all the book stores, book clubs, readers, fans and every person who has ever read anything I've written, I say thanks. None of this would be possible without you.

To those who still don't get it . . . I guess I'll have to keep on reminding you:

I don't fight, I write, so make me, please!

—*Stephanie F. Johnson,
author of Desperate Sisters*

Habakkuk 2:2–3
God is no joke, believe that!
Now I know, after all this, there was a purpose
behind all the DRAMA!

Dedication

This book is dedicated to the John L. LeFlore Magnet High School of Communication and Performing Arts Class of 1991

If I could go back to my high school years, and relive them all over again, I would not change a single, solitary moment. It was the most perfect, most entertaining, most enjoyable four years in my entire life. Thank you all for the moments, the memories and most of all, the laughs!!

Orange, orange, orange, orange
Green, green, green, green, green

Go Rattlers!

Prologue

"Qianna, you got twenty minutes to get the hell back here before I—"

Yaya hit the end button on her cell phone before Jason could finish his sentence. She couldn't even believe he had the nerve to be calling her, let alone threaten her. After all she had been through the night before, a threat was the last thing she was trying to hear. She'd just returned from Los Angeles after working on a movie set for two weeks, the biggest job she'd landed since becoming a makeup artist two years ago. She was finally starting to make a name for herself.

A seven-hour flight and a thirty-minute drive for this?—I don't think so. She sat up in her bed. *He's lost his mind for real. I coulda stayed my ass in Cali and worked another day, but that's what I get for trying to surprise his ass.*

She picked up her ringing cell phone and flipped it open, not saying a word.

"Qianna, I ain't playing with you!" Jason addressed her by her first name again, as if that would make a difference.

"Oh, and you think I am?" she said calmly into the phone. "This ain't no game, and I don't know what the hell you're talking about."

"I'm talking about my shit. I can't believe you did this to my place. My CDs are all jacked up, my clothes are everywhere, and where the hell are my shoes?—I know you did this!"

"I didn't do anything, Jason. I haven't been to your place. As a matter of fact, I just flew back into town this morning. And why the hell weren't you at the airport to meet me, huh?"

"Yaya, your ass got back last night. Stop playing with me. I know you came back last night. I also know you got your car too, so drive your ass back over here . . . now!"

I know he ain't yelling at me! Please don't tell me he has the nerve to be yelling at me! I will turn this car around, drive back there, and kill his ass!

He was right about one thing—she did get her car back. Unfortunately, it wasn't in front of his condo, where she'd parked it two weeks ago before she left. Instead, she and her friend Monya spotted it in front of them as they were on their way from the airport.

"Girl, there's Jason right there, isn't it?" Monya pointed at the champagne pink Lexus two cars ahead in the lane next to theirs, the tag reading MS Q 2U.

"Yeah, that's him. He's probably going to replace all my damn gas he drove out of it while I've been gone." Yaya laughed as the car turned into the gas station. "See . . . what did I tell you? Go over there so I can see my baby. Besides, you need some gas anyway. Your car is always on *E*."

"Gas is high. Besides, you better be grateful I drove all the way out to the airport to pick you up." Monya signaled to turn into the parking lot.

"Nobody told you to run out and get an Expedition anyway." Monya checked her reflection in the mirror. "If you can't afford the gas, then you don't need the car."

"Whatever."

Suddenly, Monya stopped the SUV abruptly.

Yaya would've busted her head on the windshield if she hadn't been wearing a seat belt. "What the hell?" She looked at Monya like she was crazy.

"Uh-oh!"

"What?" Yaya looked to see what was causing her friend to act like she had seen a ghost. At that moment, she spotted her car door open, but it wasn't Jason who got out. "Aw, hell naw! Who the hell is that?"

"I don't know."

They watched the lanky, long-legged girl, scantily clad in some raggedy shorts and a tank top, get out of the car. She was chitchatting on her cell phone.

Yaya was thinking that the chick must've stolen her car. She was all set to call 9-1-1, until she noticed the girl take the keys she was holding in her hand and aim it at the car. The familiar sound of her alarm and the flashing of the taillights let Yaya know that someone had given the stranger permission to drive it.

I'm going to kill him. Yaya's eyes squinted in anger. "Ain't this a bitch," she whispered to herself. She could feel heat throughout her body. She reached into her purse and pulled out her keys. "Pull over there."

Monya frowned. "What are you about to do?"

"I'm 'bout to get my shit!" Yaya grabbed her purse. "I don't know who this chick is, and I don't care. All I want is my car."

"What about Jason?"

"What about him?"

"Don't you wanna find out if he has an explanation?"

"Nope." Yaya got out of the truck and closed the door behind her. She used her own keys to disengage the alarm and unlock the doors.

Just as Yaya got in and started the engine, the "chickenhead" girl came running out of the store, a Slurpee in one hand and a six-pack of Heineken in the other. "Stop thief!"

Feeling the stares and not wanting to beat the shit out of the girl in front of a crowd, Yaya rolled down her window. "Look, I don't know you, and I don't give a damn who you are, but this is my car."

"Your car? This ain't your car; this is my man's car! I just borrowed it to drive to the store because he had mine blocked in—"

"Your man's car? Can you read? Did you see the tag?" Yaya snickered. The situation seemed hilarious to her for some reason. "Okay, well, maybe you ought to call your man and have him drive your raggedy shit over here and get you, since it ain't blocked in anymore. Oh, and let him know Yaya's back in town and I got my ride. Get out the way before I hit you."

As the girl reached for the door, Yaya kicked the car into reverse and pulled out so fast, she almost hit Monya's truck.

"You a'ight?" Monya yelled out the window.

"Yeah, I'm cool, girl. Let's get the hell outta here!" She sped out of the parking lot.

She picked up her phone and dialed Jason's number. "Damn," she said after his voice mail picked up. She couldn't believe this was happening to her. She loved Jason with all her heart and had worked too hard and come too far to let some half-dressed, Slurpee-drinking, beer-toting trick mess things up for them.

Being with him these past three years had given her a sense of completion. He was a strong, smart, and successful man, one her mother never thought she had been capable of becoming involved with. It was Jason who introduced her to French restaurants and Broadway shows. As an investment banker, he often had to take clients and their spouses to dinner and was proud to have her by his side.

She made a U-turn in the middle of the street and headed to his house. *I'll just wait for him to come home.* She grabbed her ringing cell phone, thinking it was Jason calling.

"Yeah," she answered, irritated that it wasn't him.

"I'm just calling to make sure everything's cool," Monya replied. "Where are you going?"

"To Jason's."

"Have you talked to him?"

"No. His voice mail keeps picking up. I'm going inside to wait for him."

"Yaya, don't do anything crazy while you're there."

"I'm cool," Yaya lied.

"Qianna Westbrooke, you know how you—"

"I told you I'm cool. Look, just take my luggage to your house. I'll come by and get it later."

"Yaya—" Monya didn't have a chance to say anything else before the phone hung up.

Arriving in record time, she pulled in front of Jason's dimly lit condo and cut the engine off. She used her key to open the door and stepped inside. Putting her phone in her pocket, she flicked on the lights and looked around.

As usual, his apartment looked like a scene from a Pier 1 commercial, decorated in an array of taupe, brown, and red. His furniture even looked like it had never been sat on. The big-screen television took up most of the wall, and next to it were shelves on each side holding hundreds of CDs and DVDs, all in alphabetical order. Each time she took one out to watch it, he always warned her about putting it back exactly where she got it from. He was so damn picky about his things.

"Seems mighty funny you weren't picky when it came to my car, huh, Jason? You just let whoever drive it, right?" she said aloud, grabbing the discs and flinging all of them to the floor. The force of her arms were so strong, the discs went crashing into the glass coffee table in the center of his floor. She was stunned for a moment, knowing he was going to have a conniption when he saw the mess. But remembering the hoochie driving her car quickly brought her back to reality, and her anger returned.

She walked into his bedroom and looked around, hoping to find something. Opening his closet door, she looked down at his shoes, lined perfectly along the floor. There had to be close to a hundred pairs. Her eyes glanced up to the clothes hanging perfectly. Everything was so damn perfect. Suits were hung on one end, then dress shirts, then casual clothes, jeans, etc. Even his shirts were color-coordinated. His neatness was usually something she liked about him, but now it just made him seem anal—*An anal, cheating liar who lets chickenhead 'ho's drive my car! I'm gonna get his ass, though.*

She picked up one of his black Kenneth Cole loafers and tossed it across the room. As it landed on the side of his bed, she got an idea. She walked into the pantry and grabbed a garbage bag. She shook it open and put every single right shoe that Jason owned inside it. *You got the right one, baby!* By the time she was finished, she could hardly carry the full bag to her car.

Popping her trunk open, she hoisted the heavy bag and tossed it inside. Satisfied with her handiwork, she got back in her car and drove home.

Exhausted from the long day she had, she took a shower and climbed into bed. She cut her cell phone off and fell into a deep slumber.

The sound of her house phone woke her. Glancing at the clock on her nightstand, she saw it was after three in the morning. She was too tired and angry to deal with Jason.

Soon, the phone stopped ringing, and she took it off the hook. *I'll handle his ass tomorrow.* She turned over, turned her phone off, and went back to sleep.

When she woke again, it was after eight. She cut her cell phone on, and as if on cue, Jason called.

They had been going back and forth for an hour now.

"What took you so damn long to call me anyway, Jason? I know that hoochie called and told you I took my car."

"I tried calling your ass, but the damn voice mail kept picking up."

"I can't believe you let some trick drive *my* car."

"I ain't thinking about your car now, Qianna—I got a meeting in an hour, and I don't have no shoes to wear."

"You know what, Jason—I ain't thinking about your shoes or your meeting right now."

"Dammit, Yaya . . . you know what—I don't have time for this right now, I got something for your ass." Jason hung the phone up.

Yeah . . . whatever.

Quianna looked through her closet for something to wear. Deciding on a pair of jeans and a white tank top, she took a hot shower and quickly got dressed.

Thirty minutes later, just as she was about to walk out the door, the phone rang again.

"What the hell do you want, Jason?"

"Um . . . Ms. Westbrooke, this is Officer Crandle with the county police department. Ma'am, you have about fifteen minutes to get here and return Mr. Taylor's items, or we'll have to come and pick you up for criminal trespass, among other charges."

Qianna closed her eyes and tried to fight the nausea that had suddenly crept over her. Monya's voice echoed in her head: *Don't do anything crazy.* Regretting that she didn't listen to her friend's advice, she knew that, this time, her temper had taken her too far.

Chapter 1

I'm going to jail, Paige thought. Quincy pulled into the driveway of what used to be her home. He hadn't even put the car into park before Paige was out of the car and headed to the doorway. She reached into her purse and pulled out her keys, praying that the locks hadn't been changed.

As she slid the key into the brass knob and it turned, her heart skipped a beat. She opened the door wide and stepped inside. She looked around and noticed that nothing really looked different. But there was a different smell. It smelled like Ms. Lucille's house, a stale mixture of cheap perfume and liquor. She had rarely been to Marlon's mother's home, but the odor was distinct those times she had been inside.

She set off through the house to find her daughter Myla, and Myla's sister, Savannah. "Myla, go get me a beer out the 'frigerator!" Ms. Lucille's voice came from the den.

"Okay," Myla answered from upstairs.

Paige waited as she heard footsteps travel from Myla's room down the steps.

"Mama!" Myla squealed and ran over to her mother, hugging her tight.

"Hey, sweetie. You and Savannah, go get your stuff so we can leave. Hurry up."

Both girls looked relieved.

"Myla! I know your ass heard me! What's taking so damn long?" Ms. Lucille yelled.

Myla looked at her mother, not knowing what to do.

"And bring me a Pepsi while you're at it, and that bag of Doritos off the counter!" This time it was Kasey's voice.

"Just go get your stuff," Paige told Myla and Savannah.

The girls took off up the stairs.

Paige walked into the den.

Ms. Lucille was kicked back on the sofa, and Kasey, Marlon's new wife, was plopped in her usual spot on the chaise lounge. They were so caught up in the Lifetime movie they were watching that they didn't see Paige enter.

She loathed the sight of both women, each of whom she wanted to kill. She contemplated taking both girls without saying anything, but there was no way she was about to leave without confronting them.

"I know that both of you are lazy as hell, but number one, neither one of you pay for maid service, and two, neither one of those girls are your maid," she snapped, startling both women.

"What the hell are doing here?" Ms. Lucille sat up.

Paige could tell that she was drunk, as usual. Her flowered housedress hung open, revealing her sagging breasts; she seemed an older, more pathetic version of herself.

"I came to get my daughter and her sister, and I also came to ask what the hell possessed you to think you could give my child a damn paternity test behind my back, without my consent!" Paige screamed, her anger rising.

Kasey grunted as she raised her large, flabby body off the chair. "This is my damn house and I can do what the hell I want to do in it!"

Ms. Lucille wobbled as she took a step toward Paige. "Damn right! Don't let this heifer come in here and disrespect your house. I whooped her ass before, and I can whoop it again!"

Paige could feel herself getting warmer and warmer with each breath. "Your son ain't here to hold me down while you swing on me today, old woman."

"But I'm here and I ain't 'bout to stand here and let you disrespect my mother-in-law. I'm *Mrs.* Marlon Davis!" Kasey screamed.

"'Mrs. Marlon Davis'! Girl, please . . . Truth be told, it's your ass I really want to hit, but I know you're supposedly knocked up and I don't wanna risk catching a charge." She faced both women, prepared to rumble and hoping one of them would make the first move.

"I don't see what you're so upset about . . . unless you're afraid the test may prove something Ms. Lucille and Marlon have known all along." Kasey stared at her intensely.

"What? That Myla is Marlon's child?"

"Ha! I don't think so!" Ms. Lucille replied.

"Mama?" Myla's voice called out.

Paige turned her head and saw Myla and Savannah standing in the doorway, holding their overnight bags. "Go ahead and get in the car. I'll be right out!"

The two girls wasted no time running out of the house. The door slammed behind them.

Kasey told Paige, "Just get the hell outta here before I call the cops on you for unlawful entry and harassment."

"Call them." Paige laughed at the woman whose lips were so thick and teeth so big, she instantly made her think of a horse. *I can't believe Marlon can even look at this ugly woman, let alone marry her.* "The number is nine-one-one."

In a flash, Kasey's arm flew back, her fist headed for Paige.

Paige moved her body at an angle and caught her by the elbow before she could connect to her body then twisted her arm behind her back and pinned her against the wall.

Kasey struggled to break free. "Ahhhhhhh-hhh! You bitch!"

Ms. Lucille tried to grab Paige. "Let her go! Let her go!"

Paige tightened her grip and pinned her against the nearby wall, placing her other hand around Kasey's throat. "That may be true, but let me let you in on a little secret—that's *my* child you're messing with and if you ever, ever touch her again, I will kill you."

Her grip became so tight that Kasey's eyes began to water.

"And another thing, this is *my* house, quiet as it's kept, *my* name is on the *deed* and it *ain't* coming off. So, since you think I'm a bitch, I'm about to show you. You got thirty days to get the hell outta here, and I mean that. Now, call Mr. Marlon Davis and let him know that!" Paige released her.

Kasey began coughing and gagging.

Knowing she had gotten her point across to Ms. Lucille and Kasey, she calmly walked out, slamming the door behind her.

As she opened the car door and got in, she heard Quincy saying on his cell phone, "Yaya, I can't come right now. I'm handling a situation with Paige. Look, just take the man his stuff back, apologize, and be done with it. If you don't, you're gonna wind up in jail. Hell, from what you're telling me you did to his place, you may just go to jail anyway. I don't understand you—that was so stupid."

"Mama, what happened?" Myla asked from the back seat.

She turned to her daughter. "Nothing, baby. Everything is fine."

"Do what I told you, Yaya—I ain't got no money to bail you out behind no stupid stuff." Quincy closed his phone. He looked over at Paige. "You good?"

"Yeah, let's roll." Paige wanted to be gone before the police or Marlon showed up. As they were pulling out of the driveway, she had no doubt that Kasey and Ms. Lucille were calling.

"You sure? You're sweating and your shirt is kinda opened." Quincy pointed to her shirt, which had obviously come undone during the scuffle.

She wiped her moist brow, fastened her shirt, and smiled like nothing had even happened. "Everything all right with you?"

"Yeah, that was my little sister Qianna. She's going through some drama with her boyfriend." Quincy sighed.

"Man, your sister got drama, your girlfriend got drama—you just can't get enough, huh?"

"I swear."

She could see the worry in his face and was mad that she had added to his stress.

He turned the radio up to drown out their conversation. "My sister just gets so crazy sometimes. She has this temper, you know."

"Well, she's young."

"Twenty-three ain't all that young."

"I thought she was out of town working for a couple of weeks?" Paige asked.

"Apparently, she came back early to surprise him and found another woman driving her car. She went off and tore his house up."

"I don't blame her." Paige laughed.

"I figured you could relate. I can imagine you went off back there, huh?"

"Do you blame me? What on God's green earth would make them think they could do that and I would be fine with it?" Paige glanced at the two girls sitting in the back seat, singing along with the radio. "I tried to choke the mess outta Kasey."

"I know you didn't." Quincy shook his head. "Do you think that was wise? I'm going to have to tell you like I told Qianna—I ain't got no money to bail you out."

"Don't worry, I'm not going to jail."

It didn't take long for Marlon to start calling Paige's cell phone. She ignored his calls knowing she wanted to be alone when she spoke to him.

The opportunity presented itself, when Quincy took the girls to the store to rent some movies and video games.

"Paige, I can't believe you came over here acting crazy. What the hell is wrong with you?"

"Marlon, I'm telling you right now, the only thing I have to talk to you about is Myla. If you're not calling to discuss her, then I'm hanging this phone up."

"I am calling to talk about Myla and the fact that you stormed into my house, assaulted my wife, cursed my mother out, and just took Myla *and* Savannah, like it was all good."

"Is that what they told you, Marlon? Did they tell you why? Did the fact that they gave those girls a DNA test without permission come up, while they were giving out false details?" She yelled into the phone.

"'DNA test'?"

"You heard me—DNA test. They told the girls they were giving them a thrush test, swabbed their mouths, and told them, if it came back positive, they couldn't come back to their house anymore."

"Damn," Marlon said, quietly.

Paige knew there was no way he knew about the test. "And where the hell were you when all this went down? Why would you leave those children alone with that horse of a wife and that drunk of a mother of yours? I bet it won't happen again. Believe that!"

"What's that supposed to mean?"

"It means that neither one of them will ever get the opportunity to set eyes on those girls again, let alone be in the same room with them."

"Paige, look, I didn't know anything about the DNA test. I'll take care of that. I'm sorry."

"I know that, Marlon—that's why we're not together anymore!"

"You know I love my daughters, I wouldn't do anything to hurt them—"

"Believe me, you won't ever have the chance to. Don't worry about handling it, I already did—your wife got thirty days."

"Thirty days to what?"

"Get the hell outta my house."

"Your house?"

"That's right, my house. That house is in both our names, remember?"

"But I pay the mortgage every month. You haven't even lived here in over a year."

"So? There were some months I paid the mortgage when I did live there, and my name is on the deed—That makes it my house, and I want her to get the hell out."

"And what am I supposed to do?"

"Not my problem. I didn't say you had to get out. I said she had to go. Why should you leave? After all, you pay the mortgage."

"I can't believe you're acting like this, Paige. I thought you were better than that."

"And I thought you were too, Marlon but, I guess it's like you told me a long time ago—'Sometimes, people change.'"

Chapter 2

"Oooooooh." Yaya threw her phone down and flopped across the bed. She could not believe her brother. *"I'm handling a situation with Paige."* She didn't know who the hell Paige was, and she didn't care. What she did care about was the fact that she needed him, and he was too busy to help her. Her plan was to call Quincy and get him to take Jason's shoes over to the house. Now she didn't know what to do.

Checking her watch, she saw that she only had ten minutes to get to Jason's condo. The sound of the doorbell startled her, and she ran to see if Jason was standing on her doorstep. Luckily, it wasn't him; it was Monya.

"Girl, thank God you're here!"

"What's wrong? I tried calling you last night. Your cell and your house phone both kept going to voice mail." Monya walked into the living room.

"I know. I turned them off because Jason kept calling."

"What did he say?—Who was the chick driving your car?"

"I don't know, girl." Yaya grabbed her purse. "Come on, we gotta go."

"Go where?—Wait, what do you mean, you don't know. Didn't you talk to him?"

"Yeah." She checked her reflection in the mirror as they headed out the door. "But he didn't tell me who the girl was. He was too mad about his shoes."

"'His shoes'?" Monya looked confused.

Yaya popped the trunk and told her what happened after she got to Jason's house.

"I can't believe you, Yaya. I told you not to do anything crazy. Now what are you gonna do?"

"You're gonna take his shoes to him so I don't go to jail."

"Me? I don't think so." Monya folded her arms and shook her head.

"Monya, please?" Yaya hoisted the bag out of the trunk. "You gotta help me out. I called *Q* but he won't do it."

"Why can't you just take the shoes over there?"

"Because . . . just do it, please." Her cell began ringing, and Jason's number flashed on the screen. "I'm on my way, dammit," she screamed into the phone.

"Thanks, ma'am. I'll let Mr. Taylor know," Officer Crandle said in her nasal voice. "I appreciate your cooperation in this, Ms. Westbrooke."

"Whatever." She ended the call.

Monya was staring at her, giggling.

"I don't see anything funny."

"You are." She laughed harder, pointing at the large garbage sack.

"Monya, please do this for me—just take the shoes over to Jason's and give them to him."

"You owe me big time, Yaya." Monya reluctantly grabbed the bag.

"I know, I do. I promise; I got your brows for the next month."

"Oh, no, you got my brows for the next two months, trick, and my mani's and pedi's!"

"Deal. Call me as soon as you leave. Thanks so much, girl!" Yaya smiled. She didn't know what she would do without Monya. They had only been friends for a couple of years, but she felt like she had known her forever. Next to Taryn, she was her best friend.

"Oh, goodness, Taryn!"

"What about her?" Monya put the bag in the back of her truck.

"I was supposed to pick her up from the airport thirty minutes ago." She checked her cell phone. "I'm surprised she hasn't called."

"A'ight, I'll call you when I leave Jason's," Monya told her.

Yaya made it to the airport in record time. She parked in the short-term lot and damn near ran to the arrival gate. She scanned the brightly lit sign, searching for Taryn's flight.

This is all Jason's fault. If he hadn't had some trash driving my car, I would've been here on time to pick Taryn up.

She located the gate number and sprinted as fast as her high-heeled sandals would let her. She searched the crowd of people but didn't see her. She paused and thought for a moment. *Luggage—she's probably gone to get it already.*

Just as she took off in that direction, she heard someone calling her name, "Yaya!"

"Hey, girl, I ain't even see you." She walked over and gave Taryn a hug.

"Okay, what the hell happened to you?" Taryn frowned, looking Yaya up and down. "What is up with the wife-beater? And what the hell is wrong with your face?"

Yaya rolled her eyes. "It's not a wife-beater; it's a tank top, you jerk. And there's nothing wrong with my face."

"Yes, it is. It's totally void of *any* make-up."

"I didn't have time for that this morning," Yaya told her as they got on the moving sidewalk.

At five foot nine, Taryn was slightly taller than Yaya, but much larger. Yaya easily fit into a size eight; Taryn, on the other hand, easily fit into an eighteen. Yet, even though she was what most people considered a big girl, she was the flyest person Yaya had ever known. It was Taryn who taught her about fashion and style, when they befriended each other in the seventh grade. Each day after school, while their friends would rush home to watch Rap City on BET, Yaya and Taryn would hop off the bus and rush to Yaya's house to study *Elle* and *Vogue* magazines and try the latest hair and makeup techniques on each other.

Even today, Taryn looked as if she had stepped out of the pages of *Essence* magazine, rather than a red-eye flight from Las Vegas. Dressed in a hunter-green pantsuit with matching snakeskin stiletto pumps, and her Chanel shades covering most of her face, Taryn's short hair was curled perfectly, and the diamond hoops she wore added the perfect touch.

"Wow! Jason must've really worn you out last night, Ms. Thang. I guess your coming back yesterday was a good idea." Taryn laughed.

Yaya acted as if she didn't hear the comment. "Which luggage track is it?"

"I think they said four." Taryn lifted her Chanel shades on top of her head. "I don't have that much stuff anyway."

"Liar! You mean to tell me you went to Bermuda on a shoot and you don't have that many bags?"

"Only three." She laughed.

"So, how was the shoot?"

"It was good. Tony was kinda upset when I told him I would be cutting back because I was opening my own business, but I assured him we would still be available for the big projects."

Tony Gordon was a well-known photographer who both Yaya and Taryn worked with quite frequently. He was a lot of fun and allowed them to be creative with their work. Hearing his name almost made Yaya think twice about the decision both girls were making. They were in high demand, known as the top make-up artists in the business. Video shoots, commercials, photo shoots, movies—they had done it all and left a lasting impression of perfection on everyone they had worked with.

"I'm going to miss jet-setting with Tony." Yaya laughed.

"Believe me, we'll still jet-set with Tony, just not as much. You sound like you're about to flake out on me."

"I'm not flaking out. It's just a big step." Yaya reached for the large Louis Vuitton suitcase and made sure it had Taryn's name on it. Seeing her name, she pulled it off the moving track.

Taryn quickly grabbed the other two bags behind it. "It's a smart move, Yaya. We've been planning this for a year."

"Would you ladies like some help?" a male voice said.

They turned to see a guy smiling at them, his gold tooth flashing. Despite his ghetto-fabulous gold, he was on the cute side. He also looked all of seventeen.

"No thanks. I think we got it," Yaya told him.

"You look too good to be struggling with those bags. Come on, let a brother at least help you to the sidewalk out front. It would be my pleasure."

Yaya looked over at Taryn, who was handing him the larger of the two bags she was carrying. The guy's eyes were glued to Taryn's cleavage, and he was smiling as if it was Christmas.

This chick is crazy, Yaya thought. *What if he grabs the bag and runs with it? He's probably a crackhead trying to find something to score with.*

"You want me to take that one for you?" he asked Yaya.

"Naw, I got this one," she told him.

Taryn laughed as they exited the airport.

"Aren't you that girl that was on *Top Model*?—Tomara?"

"No, that was *Toccara*," Taryn told him. "I'm not her, but thanks for the compliment."

"I'm going to get the car. Are you gonna be all right?" Yaya said when they got outside the airport.

"She's fine. Go ahead and get the car. I'll wait with her," Goldtooth answered.

Yaya looked over at Taryn to make sure.

Her girlfriend nodded. "I'm cool."

Yaya rushed to the car, praying that the man wouldn't abduct her best friend and chop her up, making her the topic of *America's Most Wanted*. To her relief, Taryn and Goldtooth were still standing and talking when she pulled up.

"Now this is a nice car." Goldtooth whistled when she pulled up to the curb.

"Well, I certainly appreciate your help, Dante," Taryn told him as he put her bags in the trunk. She reached into her purse and took out a ten and handed it to him.

"Come on now, don't insult me like that. I can't take your money. Now I will take your number."

"I don't think my fiancé would appreciate me giving you my number now, Dante." Taryn flashed the diamond ring on her right hand at him.

"In that case, I will take your money." He stretched out his hand, laughing.

Taryn gave him the money, thanked him again, and got in the car.

"Where the hell did you get that?" Yaya grabbed her hand and looked at the ring.

"Girl, I bought it at some little jewelry shop. Isn't it fierce? Only cost me twelve hundred, can you believe that?"

"That's it? It's like two carats!"

"I know. Now this is the type of ring I want when I get engaged. All I need now is a man to go with it."

"I can't believe you bought yourself an engagement ring."

"Why not? Don't worry, I'm sure the one you're getting from Jason will be bigger."

Once again, Yaya ignored the comment about Jason, not wanting to talk about him. She was still anxious to hear from Monya, who has yet to call her back.

"Now I know something is going on," Taryn said. "What happened?"

"What are you talking about?" Yaya pretended to focus on driving.

"This is the second time I've said Jason's name, and you haven't said a word about him. What the hell did you do?"

"What makes you think I did something, Taryn? How about, it was him that did it this time!"

She proceeded to tell her about seeing the girl driving her car at the gas station, conveniently leaving out the fact that she trashed his home.

"Oh no, he didn't! I can't believe him. I'm glad you came back early. If you hadn't, you never would've known about this. I swear, I never woulda thought Jason would be cheating, though . . . and with some skeezer; that's more like Travis."

Travis Thorn was Jason's best friend and co-worker. He took womanizing to a whole nother level and often criticized Jason about his relationship with Yaya. It was one of the many reasons that she and Travis didn't get along. He often commented about the six-year age difference between Yaya and Jason, claiming that Yaya was a young girl and didn't know how to handle a real relationship.

"I don't know what the hell he was thinking," Yaya told her.

"Obviously, he wasn't thinking." Taryn sighed. "I'm sorry, Yaya. But don't worry, girl, life goes on, and believe me, it's about to get better for us. Have you talked to *Q*?"

"He's caught up in his own little drama, girl. I tried to call and talk to him about Jason and he brushed me off."

"What? *Q* brushed you off? Now, that's a first. What kind of drama does he have going on?"

"Some chick named Paige, I don't know." Her cell began ringing. She looked at it and saw that it was Monya. "Hey, what's going on?"

"Nothing, really. I took the shoes back to him. He's really pissed, Yaya. Where are you?"

"Picked Taryn up and now taking her home— what did he say?"

"I'll meet you at Taryn's."

Monya's truck was parked in front of Taryn's townhouse when they arrived.

"What's up, *T*?" Monya gave Taryn a big hug. "You have a good trip?"

"Hey, Monya, you know I did—fine dining, fine men, fat paycheck and all expenses paid—you know it don't get any better than that!"

They all laughed as they carried the luggage inside.

"Home, sweet home." Taryn flopped down on her large, plush sofa. "Yaya told me about y'all catching the girl driving her car last night. That's wild."

"Wild ain't the word," Monya said, "I wouldn't have believed it if I ain't see it for myself. Ol' girl was rolling in the Lex like it was hers."

"I'm proud of you, though, Yaya. A few months ago, you woulda went off on Jason, cutting tires, busting windows . . . something. You know that temper of yours is—"

"Oh, she did some damage. Not as much as I thought she would've done, but she got her point across. He was pissed about his shoes. The police were still there when I got there."

"Damage? Shoes? Police?" Taryn sat up. "Oh, hold on, you ain't say nothing about any of that, Qianna Westbrooke!"

"I figured she didn't since that wasn't the first thing you asked when you got out the car." Monya giggled and went on to tell the complete story.

Yaya rolled her eyes at her as she talked.

"Well, that explains the raggedy look you're rocking today. Oh, my goodness, Yaya, I know you ain't chance going to jail, when you know you had to pick me up from the airport."

"I know you were pissed after you had to wait over thirty minutes for her to get there," Monya continued.

"Yaya!" Taryn gasped.

"Monya, your ass can't hold water," Yaya hissed.

Monya was laughing so hard that tears were streaming down her face.

"*T*, shut up. Your flight was delayed anyway. And I wasn't going to jail."

"I don't know, Yaya, I got a feeling Jason was about to send the cops to your house if I wouldn'ta pulled up when I did."

"Jason better be glad *I* didn't call the cops on him about my car." Yaya folded her arms and sat on the barstool.

"He didn't even know the girl had your car, Yaya," Monya told her.

"What?" Yaya and Taryn said at the same time.

"Yep, at least not until he got a call from Travis."

"'Travis'?—What the hell did he have to do with it?" Yaya was confused.

"I shoulda known he had something to do with it."

"Well, it turns out Travis had a fight party last night at his house, which means mad chicken-heads were there, probably. Anyway, they were running low on beer, and he sent some chick to the store. For some reason, she thought the car was his. I guess the dumb broad ain't read the tag, especially since it has *MS* on it. She tells him she's never driven a Lexus before. He gets the keys from Jason and sends her on the beer run. The rest is history."

Yaya closed her eyes as she listened to Monya. *Travis . . . all this because of Travis and one of his whores.*

"Oh my God," Taryn hummed. "What are you gonna do?"

That was the exact same question that was running through Yaya's head. The problem was, she didn't know the answer.

Chapter 3

"I know you tried to knock her out."

"You know I did," Paige told her best friend, Nina. They were sitting in the living room of Paige's mother's house, waiting on her to return with Myla and Nina's niece, Jade, who Nina had custody of.

"What in the world made her think she could give those girls a paternity test?"

"Ms. Lucille, girl. She always said that Myla wasn't Marlon's child. You know her and Kasey probably had this planned for months. Marlon getting the girls on Sunday gave them the opportunity they were waiting for. It was probably their idea for him to get them, and he was too dumb to realize they were up to something."

"What did Rachel say?" Nina asked, referring to Savannah's mother.

"Savannah is no longer allowed over there— simple as that."

Nina's phone rang. "Hello, hey there. Yes . . . uh-huh . . . that sounds good . . . let me check on something, and I'll let you know . . . it was nice to hear your voice too." Nina giggled. "Bye."

Paige looked at the wide grin on Nina's face. "And who was that?"

"A friend."

"I'll bet—What friend?"

Nina smiled. "Craig. I met him at the school one day when I was picking the girls up."

"Oh, I was thinking it was Titus."

"'Titus? Don't play with me."

Paige couldn't help but laugh.

Titus was Quincy's best friend who had a crush on Nina for months. He was a nice-look-ing, hard-working gentleman who owned his own auto shop. There was only one problem—at five foot three, there was no way Nina would date him.

"I can't believe you would even go there with me, Paige."

"What? There's nothing wrong with Titus. You know he's a good man."

"That may be true, but he ain't a tall man, and Craig is!"

The door opened, and in rushed Myla, Jade, and Paige's mother.

"Hey, Mom!" Myla ran over and put her arms around Paige.

"Hey there, baby girl," Paige greeted her daughter. "How was your day?"

"It was good."

"I'm glad," Paige told her. "Hey, Mama."

"Good evening, ladies, and how are y'all doing?" Her mother hung her keys up and put her purse on the coffee table.

"We're good, Aunt Jackie," Nina answered.

"Darling, can we go play in the backyard?" Myla asked, using the nickname she had given her grandmother, when she was a toddler.

"Go ahead, but stay in the back, you understand?"

"Yes ma'am." Both girls ran out the back door.

"Myla told me you had words with Ms. Lucille again yesterday at Marlon's." Her mother sighed.

"Yeah, I did. I had words with both her and Kasey."

"Paige, why do you let them get to you?" Her mother shook her head. "You have moved on with your life, and so has Marlon. This going back and forth with Ms. Lucille is a waste of time."

"Mama, you act like I wanna go back and forth with them. Can you believe they gave the girls a DNA test behind my back? You don't think I shoulda went over there and said anything?" Paige couldn't believe how her mother was acting. It was as if she thought Paige was in the wrong.

"No, I don't. Is Myla Marlon's daughter?"

"I know you're not asking me that."

"Well then, let them give her ten DNA tests; I don't care how many tests they give. The fact that Marlon is her father will not change."

"She does have a point, Paige." Nina shrugged, looking at Paige.

"Thanks for the support, Nina. You said yourself you woulda beat them down."

"I hope you didn't go over there putting your hands on nobody." Paige's mother shot her a look.

"I defended myself, Mama, that's all. But I did tell them they have thirty days to get outta my house."

"Now, I don't blame you for that . . . especially since your name is on the deed. You should kick them out."

"No, she shouldn't. Didn't you tell me that his new wife is pregnant? And you aren't paying the mortgage, so it's not hurting you."

Paige stared at her mother. She hated the fact that she was acting as if Paige was being the unreasonable one, when it was Kasey and Ms. Lucille that were disrespecting her.

"Mama, I can't talk to you about this. I can't believe you're making me out to be the bad person here." Paige stood up to leave.

"I'm not making you out to be anything, Paige. I'm your mother and I'm trying to tell you what's right. I'm warning you—this thing is gonna turn ugly if you don't back off and leave it alone. For Myla's sake, if for no other reason."

"Well, guess what Ma—it already got ugly." Paige walked through the kitchen and opened the back door. "Myla, come on, let's go."

"Awww, Ma," Myla whined from the swingset, "just five more minutes."

Paige could feel a headache about to come on. "No, Myla, now! I'm not calling you again!"

"Let her play a little while longer. I'll bring her home." Nina walked up to Paige. "You need some alone time anyway."

"Can you believe her? You'd think she was on their side." Paige sighed.

"You know how your mom is, she just hates confrontation."

"Whatever." Paige shrugged. "At least I know where her loyalty lies in this whole situation."

"Paige, come on now, her loyalty lies with you. It always has, and it always will. She just sees the situation differently, that's all. She's looking at it as Myla's grandmother." Nina pointed over at the two girls playing. "She doesn't want anything to disrupt that little girl's childhood."

"And I do?—That's why I'm trying to protect her from Ms. Lucille and Kasey—I've got a headache. I'll see you when you get to the house."

"You're leaving?" Her mother walked back into the den. "I was about to cook."

"Yeah, my head is hurting. Nina says she'll drop her off. See you later." Paige opened the door and almost walked smack into her Aunt Gayle.

The two of them stared at each other, neither one saying a word. Moments passed and Paige's temple began to throb. "Excuse me," she said and went to step out the doorway.

The sight of her aunt's car door opening caused her to stop in her tracks. Her cousin Celeste got out. The tension became even thicker.

Celeste couldn't even look Paige in the eye as she walked by. Her cousin had caused more trouble than a little bit and had reason to feel ashamed. For some reason, Celeste had been lying to her mother and the family about dating Quincy, when, in fact, she had been dating him. Things came to a head though, when Paige called her on her lies in front of their other cousin, Meeko.

Aunt Gayle still didn't have much to say to Paige, even though it was Celeste who lied and everyone knew it. It was as if her aunt held her personally responsible for Celeste's lackluster attitude and her lack of achievement in life, and she went out of her way to try and make Paige feel bad.

Paige thought, *I got too much other stuff to be bothered with this mess.*

As soon as she got home, Paige called Quincy. She hadn't talked to him all day, with the exception of a brief conversation at lunch.

"Hey, baby. How was your day?"

The sound of his voice made her feel better instantly. "It was long. How was yours?"

"Better . . . now that I'm talking to you."

"How is the other shop coming along?" Paige asked.

Quincy was in the process of opening a new barbershop, his fourth location. He was the most ambitious man she had ever known; it was one of the many characteristics she loved about him. After leaving Marlon and their seven-year relationship, she never imagined she could feel this way about any one.

"It's going good. I think being downtown in the business district is gonna be good. Businessmen can come in on their lunch breaks and right after work to get a cut."

"It's also good because you're opening the door for more minority businesses in the district."

"I'll also be close to my baby who works at the library downtown."

"Oh, really." She laughed. "I work down there. What's her name?"

"Paige Michaels. She's a real cute girl—short hair, nice shape."

"Nice shape?" She giggled, all of a sudden getting turned on. "What's nice about it?"

"Her legs are thick, and her behind is perfect. And don't get me started on her breasts . . . umph . . ."

Paige blushed. She rolled over on her stomach and crossed her legs. She was getting hot and wanted him. "Wow, sounds like you are really feeling your girl."

"Yeah, I am."

"You should go over to her house and show her how you feel," she suggested. She smiled, thankful that she'd left Myla at her mother's. She thought about the brand-new nightie she had recently purchased at Victoria's Secret she would be changing into before he got there.

"You're right, I should." He laughed. "But I can't."

"What?" Paige squealed, her smile instantly disappearing. "Why not?"

"I have a dinner meeting with my sister and her best friend. You know they are scheming about some business venture, and I promised to hear them out."

"Oh, you did tell me you were having dinner with your sister," she said, disappointed.

"Somebody sounds like they were a little bit pressed," he teased.

"I don't think so—never that."

"Knowing my sister, this meeting won't be that long. I love her to death, but she's about as focused as a four-year-old."

"Don't say that. What if they had the same attitude about you when you said you wanted to start your business?"

"I was a little more levelheaded than Yaya is, believe that. But I will remember that while she's talking tonight."

"And keep an open mind."

"'And keep an open mind,'" he repeated.

"You're the one who said you wished she would settle down a bit. Maybe this is her attempt to do that." Paige got up and reached into her drawer, pulling out a pair of sweats and a T-shirt, rather than the lingerie she thought she would be taking out.

"Yeah, you're right. How about I come over after dinner?"

"I'll be here," she told him. "And remember, open mind, positive attitude."

"I love you," he said.

"Love you too."

Chapter 4

Yaya sat nervously across the table from Taryn as they watched Quincy walk into Jasper's. It was their favorite restaurant, and even though it was a Monday night, it was still a nice number of people.

"Calm down, Yaya, it's just *Q*. Hell, you're making me nervous," Taryn told her.

"What's up, ladies?" Her brother greeted them both with a kiss as he took his seat.

"Hey, *Q*." Yaya smiled. "You look nice."

"He always looks nice." Taryn laughed as she took a swallow of her drink.

"Ahhh, flattery will get you two everything." He laughed. "So, Yaya, you and Jason make up yet?"

"You just go straight for the jugular, huh, *Q*?" Yaya shook her head.

She'd tried calling Jason a few times, but he refused to take her calls. She figured he needed some time to cool off and would call her when he was ready to talk.

"And, no, we haven't made up."

"You will. You two always do." He smiled at her assuredly.

"That's what I told her," Taryn added.

"So, ladies, have you ordered yet?"

"Just drinks," Yaya told him. "We were waiting on you to order food."

"Then let's get this thing started. A brother's stomach is on *E*."

"All right, let's get down to business," Taryn said after they ordered their food. She pulled out a shiny black folder with a drawing on the front and passed it to him.

He reached over and began flipping through it.

"Quincy, we know about the *Q*-Masters you're opening downtown, and we think that's a brilliant idea. It's a prime spot. Success at the location is inevitable. That being said, Qianna and I would like to follow in your footsteps and open a business of our own."

"'A business'? What kind of business?"

"A nail and aesthetic salon," Taryn answered. "After Effex."

"A nail shop." Quincy looked at them.

"It's more than a nail shop, *Q*, it's a salon. We'll do brows and faces, and we'll also sell skin care products too."

"Avon?"

"No, not Avon." Yaya was getting angry. It had taken her almost a year to get the nerve to come to him with this idea, and now he wasn't taking her seriously.

"More high-end stuff, Q. Carol's Daughter," Taryn told him. "We've researched it, Q, and we know this can work."

"What about make-up?"

"We'll still do make-up. We just won't travel as much. We already have a client base built up from what we're doing now. Besides, we can also do faces in the shop."

"That's why we're calling it a nail and aesthetic salon. Monya's a certified nail tech, and so is Taryn."

"And what is your job?—You don't do nails."

"I'll be part-owner of the shop, and in addition to doing faces, I'll handle the retail portion of the salon—office manager, per se."

"Just look at the proposal, Q."

"I'll look at it. And where is the money for this project gonna come from?"

The girls looked at each other. They knew he would ask that.

Yaya took a deep breath. "We have start-up capital, but we still need you to invest and back us up, Q."

"Our goal is to have After Effex grow as large as *Q*-Masters."

Quincy sat back and folded his arms, looking from one girl to the other as they spoke. They had a positive, well-thought-out response to every question he brought up. Their homework had been done, and just as they told him, they had done their research. Instead of a whining, begging dinner he thought he would be having, it was indeed a business meeting. And two and a half hours later, when they finished, he was thoroughly impressed.

"Excuse me for a minute." Taryn stood. "I need to go the ladies room."

"So, what do you think, *Q*?" Yaya asked after she left the table. She knew he was blown away.

"I see you've really studied this, and you may just have an idea here." He flipped through the pages.

"Really? Oh, *Q*, you think so?" She gushed then tried to play it off. "I mean, I know it's a good idea."

"But, Yaya, you're talking about running a business. Are you sure you're ready for this? It's a big responsibility. You know how you like to shop. You may not be able to live the lifestyle you've been living these past couple of years. You already know you won't be able to travel on shoots every week. Have you saved anything to live off of for the next few months to a year?"

"Yes," she lied. She really hadn't thought about saving because she knew if she needed anything, she always had Jason. He was always her back-up plan whenever she ran short, which was often. For some reason, even though she made almost fifty grand a year, she still found herself in a bind ever so often. Quincy was right about one thing—her lifestyle would have to change.

"Quincy, all I'm asking for is a chance. Believe in me the same way Uncle Troy believed in you when you wanted to open your barbershop."

"But, Yaya, I went to school and got a degree in business. I knew what I was getting into. I had been planning to open Q-Masters for years. It was my dream, and I prepared for it."

"And After Effex is Taryn's and my dream, Q, we've prepared for it. Just because we didn't go to college and don't have degrees saying we went to class for four years, doesn't mean we want it any less than you did. Guess what, Q—you own four barbershops and you suck at cutting hair."

"Hold up, hold up, hold up—"

"No, just listen. The fact that you can't cut hair has nothing to do with your success. You're a great businessman. You hired the best barbers and make mad money off them. All I'm saying is, this is the same concept. We have the best nail techs and make-up artists in the business, but we need you to help us make money for ourselves. We know it'll work, *Q*. And with you behind us, there's no way we can fail."

Taryn returned. "Everything all right?"

Yaya sat back and waited for Quincy to respond.

"It's all good," Quincy said.

"So, what's the verdict, *Q*?" Taryn asked.

They held their breath in anticipation.

He took a deep breath and exhaled. "Fine. You're right. You both deserve the same opportunity that Uncle Troy gave me. I think you two can do this, but it's gonna take two things."

"I told you we have money, *Q*," Yaya told him.

"I'm not talking about money, Yaya—it's gonna take hard work and commitment."

"And we're willing to do both of those." Taryn nodded.

"Then I say, yes, you two can open your shop—"

"Salon!" They both corrected him.

"Salon next to *Q*-Masters." He smiled.

The girls began squealing and hugging each other.

Yaya was so happy, tears formed in her eyes. *I knew Q wouldn't let me down, I knew it. He has always had my back.*

"On McNeil Street."

They instantly got quiet, and their jaws dropped in disbelief.

Yaya frowned. "'McNeil Street'?"

"That's where your old shop is, *Q*; we wanted to open up downtown next to the new shop."

"I thought you wanted my help. I'm giving you a free building."

"We do. I mean, *Q*, come on, McNeil Street?— That's the hood!" Yaya snapped.

"And that's my most successful shop."

"We're talking about opening a high-class, sophisticated salon, Quincy. We need to be downtown. That's the clientele we're trying to attract. Not Bonquisha and Shantaniqua who want their baby daddy's name airbrushed on their nails."

"Although I am the bomb at nail tricks, in case someone does want that done." Taryn winked at him.

Quincy laughed, making Yaya even more irritated.

"That's not even funny, Taryn. Look, *Q*, we'll still have regular clients who are gonna come in to get their faces done. They aren't gonna wanna come to McNeil Street."

"Then that's their issue, Yaya. You asked me for a chance, and I'm giving you one. Do you even know how much the rent is in the building downtown? Hell, I'm taking a chance myself by going down there. McNeil Street will give you ample space to do what you need to do."

"I can't believe this. I need some air." Yaya stood up and walked out the front of the restaurant.

Her vision of a classy salon was now distorted. Quincy wanted to stick her in the center of the old neighborhood where they grew up. The building had to be older than she was. Uncle Troy bought the building years ago and used to rent offices to small companies. It was his first investment, and once Quincy opened *Q*-Masters and made it a success, he gave it to him. It would take all their start-up capital just to renovate.

Maybe this wasn't a good idea after all.

Her life seemed to be falling apart around her. First, Jason; now this. Nothing seemed to be going right.

"You okay, Yaya?"

She turned to see Taryn standing behind her. "I'm pissed, but I'm okay. I guess we'll have to wait on opening the salon, huh? Or we can always just open it somewhere else on our own, find our own location."

"Girl, please . . . we're gonna do this the way we planned. Think about it, if we can make the salon work on McNeil Street, we can make it work anywhere."

"He's just trying to be difficult, Taryn. He coulda let us open next to one of his nicer shops. He wants us to fail, that's all."

"No, I don't think so. I think he wants us to work. He thinks maybe the salon will be good for the old neighborhood too. Maybe we can bring some class to the joint." She nudged Yaya's arm. "Come on, we can do this. No time for looking down now, baby. We gotta look up. Lord knows, we're gonna need to do some serious praying if we're gonna be on McNeil Street."

"McNeil Street." Yaya looked at her best friend and couldn't help but laugh. Taryn was always an optimist.

"Ladies, I know you left me all alone so you wouldn't have to pay the check—which, by the way, I did." Quincy walked up and put his arms around both of them.

"Well, being that you have four shops and we only have one, you should be treating us to dinner." Yaya rolled her eyes at him.

"So I guess I'll meet you two at the shop in the morning so we can get started?" He smiled.

"Just let us know what time," Taryn quipped.

"Is ten-thirty good?"

"We'll be there—right, Ya?"

"Yeah, we will." Yaya sighed.

Taryn and Quincy were already at the shop when Yaya arrived the next morning. She fought off the urge to call Jason, even though she needed to talk to him now more than ever. He knew opening the salon was the most important decision she had made in her life and she needed her man in her corner. She needed his support.

Dammit, Jason, call me. She stared at her phone as she sat in the parked car, hoping that some kind of way she could telepathically reach him.

Her phone began ringing. She became excited, until she saw Quincy's name and number on the caller ID.

"You're late. Why are you sitting there?" he asked.

"I'm getting out now," she huffed at him, opening her door and stepping out of the car. She pulled her sunglasses over her face, which she made sure was perfectly made before she left the house. Even though she wasn't in the mood to get dressed and made up, she forced herself to, knowing if she didn't, she would hear Taryn's mouth all day. She straightened her cream linen pants and belted shirt and headed inside.

"Well, well, well, look who the wind blew in," a familiar voice called when she stepped into the barbershop.

She cut her eyes and tried to ignore Jarrod, the manager. She and Jarrod had graduated from high school together. He was voted class clown and still wore the title proudly.

"What up, Ms. Thang? *Q* tells me we're about to be neighbors. Welcome to the neighborhood."

"Whatever, Jarrod." She brushed past him. "Hello, everyone else."

"Hey, Yaya. What up, Yaya," the other barbers greeted her.

She knew most of them, like she did Jarrod, from school. "Where's Quincy?"

"In the back"—Jarrod aimed the clippers he was using in the direction of the office—"making plans for your new salon with *T*, new neighbor."

Yaya walked to the back, where she found Quincy and Taryn talking. Taryn was holding her leather-bound note-pad, and Quincy was measuring something with a tape measure.

"Good morning."

"Hey there, girl. That pantsuit is fierce. I love it." Taryn winked at her.

"Hey, Yaya, check this out."

Quincy led them out the back door of the barbershop, into the back of the other side of the building, which was now being used as storage and would somehow become their salon. They showed her the layout he and Taryn had come up with so far. Despite it being dark and unappealing, it did have more than enough space for the salon.

"It's bigger than I thought," she said.

"I told you." Quincy smirked.

They walked through, continuing to make plans and taking notes.

By the time they finished, Yaya's initial excitement had returned, until he told her, "I'll have a door cut right here so people can walk through both shops."

"Oh, no, I don't think so."

"Why not?"

"I don't want my customers being harassed by Jarrod and your rowdy barbers," Yaya huffed. "It's bad enough we have to be next door. Now you want them to be able to just walk over whenever they feel like it?"

"I have to agree, *Q*." Taryn nodded. "You know they can get loud over there."

"Fine. Suit yourself." Quincy shrugged. He took his cell phone out of his pocket and dialed. "I already talked with a guy yesterday and showed him your layout; he should be here any minute."

"I hope that was a professional contractor and not some jackleg who rolls thru every week, and gets a haircut," she said.

"He was professional enough to do my other shops and install the flooring in your condo when you wanted me to have it done."

"I'm not saying that, *Q*. I mean, there are certain things we want to have done, and I just wanna make sure he can do it."

"And I'm sure if he's done work for Quincy, he can do it for us." Taryn laughed nervously. "Excuse us for a minute, *Q*, we need to step out back and talk." Taryn whisked Yaya out the back door. "What is your problem? Why are you being difficult?"

"I'm not trying to be difficult, Taryn. I just wanna make sure we're on point with this. I need for *Q* to understand this isn't some little home project that he's gonna pass off to one of his boys."

"He's not trying to do that. He's trying to help us . . . something we asked him to do. Lose the attitude, Yaya. I'm trying to—" Taryn stopped mid-sentence.

Yaya turned to see what caught her attention. Walking out the back door was the finest man Yaya had ever laid eyes on. He stood about six foot four and weighed about 245 pounds. Dressed in a pair of jeans and some worn-out Tims, his physique was immaculate. The cut of his chest and arms was like that of a Greek God.

His caramel skin was smooth, and there was no hair on his face or head.

"Now you see the difference between a wife-beater and a tank top." Yaya kept her eyes on the beautiful specimen coming toward them.

"Yeah, I do," Taryn mumbled.

"Excuse me, I'm looking for *Q*. They told me he would be back here." His deep voice made Yaya shiver.

She pointed. "Uh, he's on the other side, through that door."

"Thanks." He smiled at them, his teeth just as perfect as the rest of him.

They continued to watch him until he walked inside.

"Oh, God, he's fine. And you wanted to hire a professional. I can't breathe." Taryn began fanning herself.

"*Fine* ain't the word," Yaya told her.

They walked back inside.

"Lincoln Webster, this is my sister, Yaya, and her partner, Taryn Green."

"Nice to meet you, ladies." Lincoln reached and shook both of their hands. "I think this place is gonna be nice. From what *Q* showed me, your design concept is unique, and you can do a lot with it."

"Do you think you'll be able to handle the job?" Taryn asked in a husky voice.

Yaya shook her head, tickled by her friend's obvious attempt to flirt.

"Oh, no doubt." He smiled.

"I can't wait to get started." She smiled.

"I'm just as excited."

"Well, how much is this gonna cost and when do you think you can get started?" Yaya interrupted, bringing them back to reality.

Taryn shot her an ugly look.

"Well, let me get an estimate on the materials you're gonna need. Everything should pretty much be reasonable, depending on the fixtures you all want. But I have a guy who can get you a deal on that too. The construction on your brother's shop downtown won't be finished for a while, so that gives us a little time. I say we can pretty much begin gutting the place as early as tomorrow."

"Are you serious?" Yaya's eyes widened. "Wow, so soon."

"How long do you think it's gonna take to finish?" Taryn asked.

"A month, maybe sooner." He looked over at Quincy.

"Sounds good to me," Quincy said. "Well, ladies, we are now standing in what will soon be After Effex."

Yaya's emotions ran from utter happiness to sheer panic. In one way, she was elated that this was really happening, in another, she couldn't help but wonder if she was ready for it. One thing was for sure—she had to make up with Jason because there was no way she could do it without him.

Chapter 5

"He is so beautiful." Paige caressed the baby's tiny head. Meeko and Stanley had just arrived home with their newborn son, Isaiah. "As long as no one calls him *Precious*, I'm good," Meeko told her.

"Yeah, you know when they call babies *Precious*—that means they're trying to be nice and not call them ugly." Paige laughed.

"That's not true. My mother always said I was a precious baby," Stanley told them.

"I rest my case," Meeko teased. "I'm just kidding, baby. You know you'll always be precious to me, honey."

"I don't have to stay here and take this. Come on, son." He reached and carefully took the baby from Paige's arms. "We can go into your room and bond without the sarcasm. You two need anything?"

"We're fine, sweetie." Meeko smiled at him.

He leaned down and kissed her on the cheek.

"Your mama did some serious praying for you," Paige said when he left the room.

"What are you talking about?" Meeko sat back on the bed, wincing.

"Still sore?"

"Just a little. The doctor said I can only take Tylenol because I'm breast-feeding."

"What? Not you?"

"Shut up—it's what's best for my son." Meeko stuck her tongue out. "So what makes you say my mother prayed for me?"

"Come on, Meeko, look at your life—you married a good man, live in a mansion, and just had a beautiful son—it had to be because of your mother."

"Why couldn't it be because of my praying for myself?"

"Please. Praying was the farthest thing from your mind when you met Stanley."

"You're tripping. And you're just as blessed as I am. You have a beautiful daughter and a good man. Don't you wanna marry Quincy?"

She thought about that question. "I don't know Quincy well enough to say I'm ready to marry him. We just started dating really."

"Aren't you in love with him?"

"Of course, I'm in love with him."

"But you don't wanna marry him."

"I didn't say that. Stop putting words in my mouth." Paige looked up and saw Celeste standing in the doorway.

"Sorry, I didn't mean to interrupt. Mama and I just stopped by to check on you." Celeste shrugged.

Paige stood up. "I'll call you later. Take care."

"Paige, don't leave, you just got here," Meeko pleaded. "Come on, I just had a baby. I should be celebrating with my family. My entire family."

"You're right, Meeko. That's why I'm leaving—so other members of your family can celebrate with you."

"Paige, please. I'm not trying to cause any trouble," Celeste told her.

"Celeste, I'm not trying to even talk to you, okay. Just let it go. Just because we're cousins doesn't mean we have to be friends—that ain't happening. I'm no longer gonna front like I even like you, okay." Paige cut her eyes at her.

"What do you want from me, Paige? I apologized more than enough times." Celeste had the nerve to have tears in her eyes.

"And? I accepted it. So what more do *you* want from me?"

By now, Celeste was straight-up bawling.

"Paige, don't be like that," Meeko said quietly.

"Like what? Here we go once again—Celeste is the victim and everyone is to feel sorry for her. You know what, you should be an actress." Paige walked out. She knew she was moments away from going off.

"You're leaving?" Stanley almost startled her when she got to the bottom of the steps. Standing next to him was Aunt Gayle and Meeko's mother, Aunt Connie.

"Yeah, I gotta get back to work."

"Good," Aunt Gayle commented.

"Excuse me," Paige snapped.

"I said, 'Good'—I ain't stutter. The last thing Meeko needs in her house is a bunch of tension caused by you. Whenever you're around anyone in this family, they feel like they have to walk on eggshells because they're afraid you're gonna go off."

"Aunt Gayle, that's not true," Stanley said.

"It is true. Before we go to anyone's house, we have to ask if Paige is there before coming over. The only reason we ain't call over here is because I didn't want the phone to wake the baby, Stanley. If I woulda known she was here, I woulda waited 'til she left."

"That's not true, Aunt Gayle, and you know it. You were just at my mother's house yesterday, and I was there."

"And when we got there, you left."

"I was walking out the door when you were walking in." Paige shook her head. "Aunt Connie, Stanley, I'll see you all later."

"Paige, now you know you were wrong for disrespecting your aunt like that this afternoon," her mother said when she went to pick Myla up. Her mother was working in the flowerbed in front of her house.

"Mama, I wasn't disrespectful at all. Aunt Gayle was straight-up lying, saying I was causing tension in the family. I haven't done anything."

"You're not making things any better either. I know that Celeste is a little upset because you are dating Quincy, but that's no reason for you to be exchanging words with your aunt."

"Mama, I didn't exchange words with anyone. As far as Celeste is concerned, I don't have any words for her. She lied, she got caught, and I'm over it."

Nina pulled into the driveway and got out. "Hey there."

"Hey, girl." Paige sighed.

"I'll go inside and get the girls," Paige's mom said.

"Did I interrupt?"

"No, she's just tripping about Celeste and Aunt Gayle, that's all. I don't understand why, though."

"I don't know either. They were all acting kind of strange after you left though. Your aunts went into the kitchen and were whispering. Celeste just sat on the sofa, barely saying two words. I don't know what's going on."

"Me either. Celeste is probably acting like she is suicidal, since I'm dating Quincy. I don't care—that girl has some serious issues, and she needs to get checked out," Paige told her.

"Hey, do you think you can keep Jade this weekend?"

"Sure. What do you have going on?" Paige smiled.

"A romantic evening for a change." Nina batted her eyelashes.

"With who? Or do I even need to ask?"

"Craig, of course."

"So . . . this thing with him is getting serious?"

"He's nice and easy to talk to. He makes me laugh. I like him."

Paige looked at her best friend. Nina had a twinkle in her eye that Paige hadn't seen in a while. "I'm happy for you. I would love to take Jade this weekend while you get your groove on."

"I ain't say all that, Paige."

"You ain't have to say it. I can see it in your eyes."

Nina's phone began to ring. "Speak of the devil . . ."

The girls came running out of the house. Paige told her mother and Nina good-bye, and they headed home.

"Mom, you told Daddy I couldn't come to his house anymore?" Myla asked as she drove.

"Not for a little while, until I get some things straight."

"Ms. Kasey says that you're kicking them out because you want our old house back."

"What?" Paige glanced over at her daughter. "What are you talking about? When did you talk to Ms. Kasey?"

"This afternoon. She called to tell me hi. Then she said that they have to find a new house because you are kicking them out."

This is not happening to me. There is no way that crazy bitch is calling my child when I told her to leave her alone. She's just doing this to mess with me.

Paige reached and grabbed her cell phone. She dialed her mother's number. "Mama, did Kasey call and talk to Myla this afternoon?"

"I don't know. I've been in the yard working," her mother answered nonchalantly.

"I can't believe this. I'm going to kill her!"

"Paige, calm down. So what if she did call Myla?—that's her stepdaughter, you should be glad that she's making the effort to build a relationship with her."

"That's what you think she's doing?—building a relationship with Myla? She barely says two words to Myla when she's at the house, other than making demands to clean up or do some other household chore. She's doing this to be funny, Mama." The fact that her mother was acting like it was no big deal only made Paige angrier. "Bye, Mama."

"Did I do something wrong, Mommy?" Myla asked.

Paige looked over and saw the fear in her daughter's eyes.

"No, baby, you didn't do anything wrong. I don't want you talking to Ms. Kasey anymore, you understand? If she calls, you don't talk to her."

"Why not?"

Paige leaned her head back. She hated the fact that Kasey was putting her child in the middle of this drama. "Because it's just not a good time to be talking to her, that's all. Understand?"

"Mom," Myla said, causing Paige to look over again, "are you sure I didn't do anything wrong?"

"Yes, baby, you are fine." Paige smiled.

"Then can we go to McDonald's for dinner?"

As angry as she was and as frustrated as she was with her family at that moment, there was nothing better Paige could think of than having dinner with her daughter at McDonald's.

Somehow, dinner turned into a stop at the mall, and by the time Paige and Myla made it home, it was dark.

"Myla, didn't I tell you to cut that TV off this morning before we left." Paige noticed the flicker of light coming from the living room.

"I did, Mommy." Myla shrugged.

"Obviously, you didn't." Paige cut the truck off and opened the door. "Grab those bags when you get out."

"Okay."

Paige fit her keys into the door and turned the knob. As she stepped inside, she saw that, not only did Myla leave the TV on, but her purple Bratz blanket was lying on the floor in front of the sofa. "Myla Seymone Davis, I'm going to beat your behind!"

"What did I do, Mom?"

"You left the TV on, your blanket on the floor." Paige reached over and picked it up.

"I didn't leave that there, Mom."

"Then who did?" Paige turned and asked.

"I did."

They turned to see Camille, Marlon's sister, walking out of the kitchen, eating a bowl of cereal.

"Surprise!"

Chapter 6

Yaya stood outside Jason's door and rang the doorbell. She was tempted to try her key to see if it worked, but she didn't want to take the chance of being disappointed if it didn't. She waited a few moments and rang the bell again. She knew Jason was home because she followed him from work. She had given him enough time to take a shower and grab a beer from the fridge, and imagined he was about to stretch out on the couch and watch *SportsCenter*. After still not getting an answer, she proceeded to knock loudly.

"Jason, come on, I know you're in there," she called out. She tiptoed and peered into the small window. She could see him walking around. "Open the door, Jason. I need to talk to you."

"Go away, Yaya. We don't have anything to talk about."

"Yes, we do. Come on, open the door!" She knocked even harder.

"No, get away before I call the police . . . again!"

"Jason, stop tripping. Open the door, please!"

"Leave me alone, Yaya. I told you I don't have anything to say to you."

"But I have something to say to you, Jason. It's been a week. I keep calling you, and you won't answer your phone."

"Because I don't wanna talk to you. Leave, Yaya. I mean it."

Yaya was mad. This was not turning out like she planned. She thought she would come over, Jason would let her in, she would apologize, he would forgive her, and they would celebrate her news about the opening of After Effex with a glass of wine and a night of lovemaking. Frustrated, she took a chance of putting her key into the lock and turning the knob. She smiled when the door opened.

"Damn, I forgot to change that lock," Jason huffed when she stepped inside.

"You know you didn't want to do that anyway." She walked over and faced him.

"What the hell do you want?" He turned away from her.

"I want you, Jason. I want to talk to you. I'm sorry about last weekend. You can't really blame me though, can you?" She took a seat on the sofa and made herself comfortable. She looked around and saw that his CDs and DVDs were lined up neatly once again. He had even replaced the shattered glass of the coffee table with a new one.

"Yaya, please, I've had a long day, and I'm really not in the mood to deal with this."

"None of this would've happened if it wasn't for Travis. I don't even know why you hang out with his trifling ass anyway."

"This has nothing to do with Travis, Yaya."

"It was Travis that had some 'ho' driving my car without my or your permission, wasn't it?"

"It wasn't Travis that came over here and vandalized my home though, Yaya. It was you."

"Okay, you're right about that part. I was wrong, but you can understand why I was upset, Jason. Think about if you woulda seen another guy driving your Range Rover when I was supposed to be driving it. How would you have reacted?"

"I wouldn't have gone to your place and did what you did. That was crazy. Crazy, Yaya." He took a swallow of his beer.

"I know, and that's why I came over to apologize, Jason."

"Fine." He turned and stared at her.

He looked so good wearing nothing but a pair of red basketball shorts and some Adidas flip-flops. She let her gaze drift from his eyes all the way down his body, pausing to admire his well-defined chest and abdomen. Her eyes landed on his crotch.

"I'm waiting."

"Huh?" She turned her attention back to his face.

"You said you came to apologize, so apologize and leave." He leaned on the counter.

She spotted his bottle of Heineken right behind him. *I know him so well.* "Jason, I'm sorry. I overreacted, and I'm sorry." Yaya stood up and walked over to him, placing her hand in the middle of his chest. "Will you accept my apology?"

He put his hand over hers and removed it. "Yes, I do, but I can't deal with this anymore. It's too exhausting for me."

Yaya frowned. "What are you talking about, Jason?"

"This-this back and forth . . . the tantrums . . . I'm just tired. I told you that the last time this happened."

"Jason, that was almost two years ago. With the exception of last weekend, we've been good; you even said that yourself." Yaya was shocked by this reaction. Jason had always forgiven her, and they would always pick up where they left off.

When they first started dating, she would often let her jealous nature get the best of her. Throwing objects, screaming, and going off was just a part of their relationship, until the incident that left her foot fractured, and a hole in Jason's wall where she'd kicked it. He had given her an ultimatum—either she calm down or it was over. Slowly, she evolved into the calm, professional woman he desired.

"Well, maybe I was wrong," he told her.

"No, you weren't, Jason. Baby, you know how we are . . . how I am."

"Yeah, I do, Yaya, but I know that I'm tired too. I think maybe we need a break from this, from each other."

"Jason, baby, please. I need you. Things are happening for me. Taryn and I are opening the shop. I mean, I-I need you with me. I need you to talk to, to be there for me." Yaya began crying uncontrollably. "I love you, Jason. I can't do—"

"Yaya, stop. Don't do this." Jason looked at her strangely, causing her to cry harder.

"Oh God, please help me, Jason." She began shaking. "I love you, Jason. We love each other. I'm sorry. I swear it'll never happen again. I won't lose my temper."

"Yaya, listen to me." Jason grabbed her shoulders. "Calm down and listen."

Yaya shook her head. "No, this is not happening. You cannot leave me, not now."

"It's not about me leaving you; it's about taking a step back and re-evaluating this entire situation. God, look at us—this is what I'm talking about—look!"

Yaya stopped. Her chest rose and fell with each breath she took. Her heart was pounding, and she could taste vomit in her mouth. Jason was right—she was out of control. Her hands were trembling as she brought them to her face. She caught her reflection in the mirror hanging on the wall above the sofa. Mascara was streaming down her face, leaving a black trail down her cheeks. How had it come to this?

She was embarrassed, not just for now, but for all the times she had acted like this before. This time was different, though. All the other times, after she had promised never to do it again, Jason would pull her into his arms and tell her everything would be fine. He'd lecture her, and they would move on. This time, he just stared.

"I'm sorry," she whispered and turned away, unable to face him.

Jason walked out of the room and returned with a wet cloth. He handed it to her, but she didn't move.

"Yaya, come on."

She took the washcloth and wiped her face. "I guess I look pretty pathetic, huh?"

"I've seen you look worse," he said, smugly. "Look, Yaya, I think we need to take some time apart."

"But—"

"No, listen. It's a stressful time for both of us right now. I got shit going on at work, and you're talking about trying to open a business with Taryn—"

Tears began to form in her eyes again. "That's why we need each other the most right now, Jason."

"No, Yaya, I need some time to myself, to think things through and sort through some things. You and I are so chaotic right now that it's becoming a distraction."

"So, that's it. We're over?"

"We're not over, Yaya; we're just taking a break. We'll still talk and see each other; we just won't be in each other's space."

"Jason, what are you talking about? The reason I was opening the salon with Taryn was so that I wouldn't have to travel so much and we would have more time to spend with each other, re-member?" Yaya was so confused by what he was saying. It sounded like this was something he had been thinking about for some time.

"I know, and that's a good thing. Let's just give it some time, Yaya, and see how it works out." Jason pulled her into his arms and held her tight. "I love you, Yaya, but this is just too crazy for me to be dealing with right now."

Yaya closed her eyes and tried to tell herself that this was a nightmare that she would be waking up from in a few moments. Jason was the love of her life, and she didn't know what she would do without him. It may have been Taryn that taught her about style and fashion, but it was Jason who taught her about sophistication. Long gone were her days of jeans and T-shirts. Jason filled her closet with designer suits and dresses and the Jimmy Choo shoes to match. It was because of Jason that she turned heads when she walked onto the sets, rather than the hot models and singers who were supposed to be the center of attention. Now, he no longer wanted her, and she didn't know what she was going to do.

"I guess I need to go then," she told him.

"Call me to let me know you made it home." He walked her to the door.

"No, I'll be okay." She opened the door to her car. She felt like a zombie as she got in.

"Yaya, you know I love you, right?" He leaned into the car and stroked her hair.

She nodded without looking at him. *You love me, but you don't want me.* "Good-bye, Jason." She closed her door and waited until he went back into the house before backing out the driveway and crying all the way home.

Chapter 7

Camille's arrival at her house didn't come as a surprise to Paige. They had always been close, from the moment they met. Camille had never really had a close relationship with her mother, mainly because Ms. Lucille remained intoxicated most of Camille's life. Unlike her mother, Camille welcomed Paige into the family, and Paige embraced Camille as the younger sister she never had.

"Aunt Cam!" Myla dropped the bags on the floor and ran to hug her aunt.

"Let me guess—no one knows you're here, right?" Paige asked.

"Nope, and I'd like to keep it that way, if possible." Camille grinned sheepishly.

"Cam, you know how things are between me, your brother, your mother, hell, his new wife."

"You act like things between me and them are hunkydory." Camille plopped down on the sofa, pulling the blanket over her legs, "Come on, Paige. I'm not going to summer school, and I didn't have anywhere else to go. I'm not staying there with that fat, lazy, so-called wife of his, and there's no way I'm going to spend my summer cleaning up after her and sobering up my mother."

"Why didn't you mention this when we talked yesterday?" Paige sat on the other end of the sofa and faced her.

"Because I wanted to surprise you."

Paige didn't mind having Camille at her house, but the fact that Camille didn't want anyone to know she was there made her uneasy. She knew that once Ms. Lucille and Marlon found out, there would be even more trouble, and more trouble with the Davis clan was the last thing she felt like dealing with.

"Camille, you've got to let Marlon know you're here."

"But, Paige—"

"I'm not saying tonight, but at some point they're gonna find out and think I had something to do with it."

"No, they won't. Look, I'll tell Marlon in a few days, I promise. So, can I stay here for the summer?"

"Yes!" Myla nodded in excitement.

Paige shook her head at the two of them. "Myla, get ready for bed while I talk to Aunt Cam."

"Mom—" Myla started to protest.

"Go ahead, Myla, and I'll come up in a few minutes." Camille winked at her.

Myla jumped up and ran upstairs.

"Please," Camille continued to plead.

"Fine. But you have to get a job."

"I'll get one, that's no problem. Plus, I'll help out with Myla, so you can go out and have some fun this summer."

Hearing that, Paige realized that having Camille live with them for the summer was an even better idea than she'd first thought. She and Quincy really hadn't spent a lot of time together over the past few days, with his putting the final touches on the new shop and helping his sister open her salon.

"Speaking of fun this summer . . . how is Mr. Quincy?" Camille asked.

"He's good. He's opening another barbershop next weekend right downtown near the library," Paige told her.

"Can we say *lunchtime quickies*?" Camille giggled.

"Watch your mouth." Paige threw a pillow at her.

"Maybe I can get a job at the barbershop as a receptionist. I can see myself spending my days watching fine men come in and out all day." Camille laughed.

"Camille Davis, I don't know what's gotten into you, but you sound like you've gotten a little hot in the pants your freshman year of college. I don't know if I can handle you this summer." Paige was amused by the once shy introvert now giggling about boys.

"Don't worry, Paige, you know my bark has always been bigger than my bite. Unfortunately, I'm still a virgin." She sighed.

"Good. And I plan for you to stay that way until you're married."

Myla's voice came down the steps. "Aunt Cam, I'm ready!"

Camille put her now empty cereal bowl on the table and stood up. She folded the blanket and tucked it under her arm then picked the bowl up. "Thanks, Paige. You're the only person in my life I have that I can trust. If it wasn't for you and Myla, I wouldn't have anyone."

Paige watched her walk out of the room and prayed that she'd made the right decision by allowing Camille to stay.

"Hey, Paige," Camille said, when Paige answered her desk phone.

"Hey, Cam. What's going on?"

"Tia has been trying to reach you. She's called the house twice this morning."

"Your cousin?"

Tia was Marlon's cousin and the mortgage broker who helped them to buy a house. She was really nice, and Paige liked her a lot.

"Yep. I didn't tell her who I was. She thinks I'm the babysitter." Camille laughed. "I didn't want to chance her telling Marlon or Lucille she talked to me."

"I wonder what she wants."

"I don't know, but you may want to give her a call." Camille gave her the number.

Paige called it immediately. She hoped nothing happened or no one died. "Hey Tia, its Paige."

"Hey, Paige. I've been trying to reach you. Marlon brought me your paperwork, but I need some more info from you."

"'Paperwork'?"

"Yeah . . . to refinance the house. I can probably get it done quickly, girl. You all have a lot of equity built up and having it as rental property is a smart idea."

"Tia, I don't know what you're talking about."

"Huh? What do you mean?"

"I don't know anything about refinancing the house."

"Paige, I'm sorry. I know you and Marlon aren't together anymore, but I thought this was a decision you knew about. I mean, you'd have to know, for this to go through, because the house is in both your names. Look, don't worry about it. I'll call Marlon and—"

"No, I'll call him. Give me a couple of days and I'll get back with you. Don't say anything to Marlon about having spoken to me."

"That's fine. I can tell him my appraiser is backed up and it'll be awhile."

"Yeah, tell him anything. He'll believe it, coming from you. Thanks for calling. By the way, how did you get my home number? I know Marlon didn't give it to you."

"Funny thing. I called his cell and office numbers and couldn't get in contact with you. I knew you had moved and took the chance that your number may be listed, and you were."

"Thank God for small favors. I'll talk to you later."

Paige couldn't believe Marlon tried to sell the house behind her back. *How could he be dumb enough to think he could do that? Of all the crazy, low-down things he could possibly do* . . . She was livid. That house was an investment that she and Marlon had made together for their children. She hated the fact that she didn't listen to her father when he told her to think carefully before buying it with Marlon because they weren't married. In her mind at that time, she thought she would be Marlon's wife soon. Things didn't quite work out that way, and even when she moved out, she didn't think about what would happen to their house. *Daddy was right—I should've listened to him a long time ago.*

"Hey, you ready to go to lunch?"

She looked up to see Quincy standing in the doorway.

"I'm too pissed to eat," she told him.

"What's wrong? What has Celeste done now?"

"It's not Celeste, it's Marlon." She turned off the computer and grabbed her purse.

"And what has the ex-love of your life done now?" He smiled.

"You're trying to be funny—He's trying to re-finance the house," she told him as they walked out of her office and into the quiet library. The loudness of her voice caused the few lunchtime visitors to look up. She knew she was out of order, but she was too mad to care. Besides, she was the boss.

"What house?" Quincy asked. They walked over to his silver Acura and he opened the door for her.

"Our house."

"The house you used to live in?—that house?"

"Yes, that house."

"Oh, is that a bad thing?" He glanced over at her.

"It is, when he's trying to do it behind my back."

"He ain't tell you he was selling it? Now that's messed up, I ain't lyin'."

"I can't believe he would be so low-down and stupid. I know his mama told him to do it, and he probably listened to her like a dumb ass. That's why I told them to get the hell out my house anyway, her and her fat, nasty daughter-in-law."

"You told them to get out of *your* house?" Quincy pulled into the parking lot of Applebee's.

Paige rolled her eyes at him. "Your repeating everything I tell you isn't helping any."

"I'm just trying to get a full understanding of what's going on."

"Remember when we went to the house and got the girls?" she asked him after they were seated and placed their orders.

He nodded. "Yeah, Kasey gave them the test."

"Right. Well, while I was there, I gave Kasey and Ms. Lucille their thirty-day notice."

"You told them they had to get out? Doesn't Ms. Lucille have her own house?"

"I don't know if she does or not. I know she's been staying at mine, along with that cow, and I want them out."

"So you're kicking them out your house?"

"Well, technically, I can't kick Marlon out because his name is on the deed." Paige took a sip of water.

"But you want his mother and his pregnant wife to go?"

"Exactly."

"Do you really think that makes sense? I mean, come on now, Paige, be reasonable."

Quincy was being just as aggravating about the situation as her mother was. It seemed as if everyone was on Marlon's side.

"I *am* being reasonable. His mother constantly disrespects me, along with his wife, and I'm supposed to let them live in me and Marlon's house? You don't see the wrong in that?"

Quincy sat back and stared at her for a moment. "What I do see the wrong in is you still thinking the house is yours and Marlon's. It's just another thing that ties you to him and you don't want to let go."

Paige frowned. "That's crazy."

"No, it's not. Marlon is married and has a new baby on the way. You don't live there. You said yourself you never had to pay the mortgage. If he wants the house, let him have it."

"No, I'm not letting him have anything."

"You're not even being rational."

"Why should I be the rational one? Is he being rational by going behind my back?"

"You know you legally can't kick Kasey and his mom out. You only own half the house, and Maron owns the other half *and* he lives there. If he gives them permission to live with him, they can stay. You think he's too stupid to realize this and consult a lawyer?"

Quincy sounded like the voice of reason, something she really didn't feel like hearing at that moment.

"I know all of that Quincy 'Matlock' Westbrooke. Thanks. You know what—it's not even worth discussing. Let's just enjoy our lunch."

"Cool with me." Quincy told her.

As soon as she returned to her office, she dialed Marlon's cell number and got his voice mail. It took everything within her not to leave a nasty message. She decided to be smarter than that. Instead, she left a pleasant one. "Hey, Marlon, it's me, Paige. I was just thinking about you. Give me a call when you get a chance. Talk to you soon. Bye."

Chapter 8

"Did you see the car Titus has for sale outside his shop?" Monya asked, as they unloaded stuff out of the car and took it inside.

The salon was coming together nicely. True to his word, Lincoln had the place gutted, painted, and floored in a matter of days. The plumbing had been done, and things were moving along swiftly. They walked inside to the sounds of Babyface blasting from the boom box.

"No, I didn't see it," Yaya answered.

"Girl, how about—it's a gold Benz. I don't know what year, but it's got your name written all over it. You better call him and see what's up."

"Yeah."

Any other time, Yaya would have had her brother's best friend, Titus, on the phone in minutes, trying to find out about the car he was selling at his body shop. She didn't really care about anything these days, feeling as if she was going through the motions.

She missed Jason terribly. She thought that, by now, they would have at least spent some time together. She had only talked to him twice, since he'd decided, "I need some space."

It was hard going home after a long day of preparing for the salon's opening and not being able to share it with him. She wanted to get his opinion about the decisions she was making, and more than anything, she needed his support, not to mention the warmth of his body next to hers.

"Uh, I thought we agreed no major purchases until we've been open for a year," Taryn said. "Unless I come across a convertible Jaguar for a steal, that's the only exception."

"Whatever," Yaya said.

"Yaya, I need for you to get some excitement about you, girl." Taryn looked up from the mirror she was hanging. Since meeting Lincoln, all of a sudden, she was always present during the entire reconstruction process of the salon. "How does that look?"

"It looks fine," Yaya said, barely paying her any attention. She placed the bags in the middle of the floor and walked off.

"Yaya, don't leave them there! Put them—"

Yaya walked back out the door. The parking lot was crowded with cars and trucks of guys who were waiting their turn at *Q*-Masters. A little boy was going back and forth, trying to do tricks on a skateboard.

She opened her trunk and took out more bags. She closed the trunk and turned to go back in the building.

CRASH!

Before she knew it, she was on the ground along with all the bags. The palms of her hand were killing her. She shook her head to make sure she was still conscious. As she looked up, she saw what she had tripped over and who it belonged to. The red skateboard lay near her legs.

"Sorry," the little boy told her.

Infuriated, Yaya got up. She ignored the blood coming from the palm of her hand and grabbed the little boy by the collar. She snatched the door of *Q*-Masters open and screamed, "Who the hell does this 'bébé kid' belong to?"

Everyone froze in their spot and stared. No one moved; it was as if they were waiting on her to say something else.

"Whose rug rat is this?" She held on tighter as the little boy tried to get away.

"Ouch!"

"Get your hands off my son."

Yaya turned to see a tall man dressed in a brown uniform approaching her.

"Does this belong to you?"

The man wore a look of anger that almost made her take a step back. "I told you to get your hands off my son."

Yaya looked down at the little boy, terrified. She didn't know if it was because of her or his father. She released his shirt, and he quickly stepped away.

"Yaya, don't come in here trippin'," Jarrod said to her.

"I ain't come in here to trip. I came in to see who was it that left their child unattended in the parking lot of my establishment, playing on a damn skateboard at that."

"Carver, didn't I tell you to leave that skateboard in the car?"

"Yes, sir." The little boy lowered his head.

"Look at me when I'm talking to you," the man demanded. "Go wait for me outside."

The little boy looked up at his father. "Yes, sir." Then he turned and told Yaya, "Sorry."

Yaya looked at him. "It's cool."

"I realize my son may have been in the wrong, but that ain't give you the right to handle him the way you did." The man's gaze fell on her bleeding hands. "And the next time you put your hands on someone else's child, you may wanna make sure your hands are clean—I like to keep my rug rat neat."

Yaya looked down at her scraped and bleeding hands.

Before she could respond, the man had walked out the door.

"Dammmmmmmnnn," Jarrod, the other barbers and the customers all said at the same time.

Yaya rolled her eyes and stormed out. She walked back over to her car, where her bags were still laying on the ground. She bent over to snatch them up.

"Let us help you with those." The man and his son reached to pick up her bags.

"No. I got it."

Either he didn't hear her or ignored her reply. Not only did they pick the bags off the ground, he reached and took the bag she was holding out of her hand.

She walked into the salon, and they followed her.

Lincoln was installing a light fixture over the mirror Taryn had hung. "What's up, little man?"

Yaya saw that he was talking to the little boy.

"Hey, Uncle Linc," he said, smiling.

"Where do you want these?" The man was still holding the bags.

"Oh, you can put them over here," Monya answered. "Not in the middle of the floor like some people."

"Your hand is still bleeding." The man placed the bags against the wall.

"I'm fine."

"What happened?" Lincoln peeked at Yaya's hand.

Carver started telling them what happened, before Yaya could open her mouth.

Yaya could see the adults suppressing smiles, and wondered why she was the only one who didn't find it funny.

Taryn shook her head. "Yaya, I know you did not do that."

"Carver, what did I tell you about running your mouth?"

"No, Daddy—Uncle Lincoln asked me what happened, and I was just telling him—I didn't tell on her or anything."

"Fitz, this is Taryn, that's Monya, and the bleeding girl who yoked your son up is Qianna, also known as Yaya. Don't worry . . . she ain't as hard-core as she thinks she is. You know Q?—that's his sister. This is their salon, After Effex." Lincoln went back to screwing the fixture. "Ladies, this is my brother, Fitzgerald, we call him Fitz."

"Nice to meet you," Fitz told them. "Well, I gotta get outta here. What you got going on later?"

"I'll be here late. Trying to get these ladies up and running by week after next," Lincoln told him. "Taryn says she's gonna hang out and help me out tonight."

"I'll stay too," Monya announced.

Taryn looked over and gave her a dirty look.

"Feel free to come by and help your bro out," Lincoln told him.

"You already got enough free labor with these three."

"Uh, make that two," Monya corrected. "You know Yaya ain't staying and doing jack."

Yaya gave Monya the dirty look this time, causing everyone to laugh. "Go to hell."

"I may come back through," Fitz said as he walked out the door.

Lincoln hopped off the ladder he was standing on. "Let me holler at you before you go, in case you don't return."

"God, I thought Lincoln was fine," Monya squealed after they walked out the door.

"Lincoln is fine," Taryn added, "but I gotta say, Fitz is sexy as hell. That man is gorgeous."

Yaya looked out the window, silently agreeing with her compadres.

Fitzgerald and Lincoln had the same height and build, but where Lincoln's complexion was the color of chocolate, Fitzgerald's was the color of honey, with grey eyes. Instead of a baldhead, Fitz had shoulder-length dreads neatly pulled back. His sex appeal was evident even in his walk.

She watched the two brothers talking and laughing in front of the Honda Accord station wagon Carver was sitting in.

"I think he looks better than his brother—what do you think, Yaya?"

"He's a'ight," Yaya lied, and turned away.

Lincoln returned and announced, "My brother wants to know what's up with you."

"Who?" Yaya asked, after neither Taryn nor Monya responded.

"You," Lincoln told her. "I don't know why."

"Because she's the bomb, that's why," Taryn told him. "Is he coming back?"

"What's up, Yaya? You betta holla at your boy . . . because he is fine." Monya giggled.

"I don't think so." Yaya looked at them like they were crazy. "You know he's not my type."

"That's exactly what I told Fitz when he asked." Lincoln laughed. "There's no way. You're not his type."

"What does that mean?" Taryn put her hands on her hip.

"I guess the same thing it means for her," Lincoln answered. "Why isn't he your type?"

Yaya was getting irritated. She was already in a funk, and they were getting on her nerves. She walked over to the small sink and began washing her hands. "Look, first of all, I have a man."

"I thought you and Jason broke up," Monya said.

"No, we didn't; we're just on a break."

"Isn't that a breakup?" Lincoln looked at Taryn.

"No, it's not. We're just taking some time apart; there's a difference. But even if I didn't have a man—which I do by the way—I wouldn't date him. For one, he's light-skinned."

"Ohhhhhh," Monya groaned.

"You both know I don't find light-skinned guys attractive, come on. And then, he has dreads, of all things—another turn-off."

"You're crazy." Taryn shook her head.

"And you both know he has the other thing that I don't do, so don't front like you don't know me better than that—never have, never will. I'm outta here." Yaya snatched a paper towel out of the dispenser and walked out without saying another word.

"What's 'the other thing' she doesn't do?" Lincoln looked at both Taryn and Monya.

"*Baby mama drama,*" Monya said.

"The moment she found out Carver was his son, any hopes he had of getting with Yaya were out the door. He doesn't have a shot in hell," Taryn added.

On the way home, Yaya drove by Titus' shop to see what Monya was talking about. Sure enough, parked in the lot was a shimmering gold Mercedes Benz C-Class, another one of her dream cars. Peering through the windows, she saw it was more than she'd imagined. It would be the perfect addition to her collection, which already included her champagne Lexus and her first car, a silver Honda Prelude coupe.

She had to have it.

She whipped into the parking lot and hopped out. "Hey, where's Titus?" She asked the guy at the counter.

"He's out of town for a minute. Won't be back for about three weeks. Can I help you with something?"

"Nope. I'll call him on his cell." She walked out.

She tried to reach Titus, but only got his voice mail. She called Q and couldn't reach him either. She looked back at the car once more. "Don't worry, baby, Mama is coming to pick you up soon."

Chapter 9

"Did you call your brother?" Paige asked, flipping through the latest issue of *Essence*.

"Yes, I did. He knows I'm here," Camille answered. She was making a big bowl of popcorn for Myla and Jade, who were upstairs deciding on a movie.

"Are you telling the truth?"

"Do you think I would lie about something as serious as that, Paige? I'm appalled that you would even think that way." Camille put her hand over her chest and gave an obvious fake gasp.

"Get over it—What did Marlon say?"

"As usual, he tried to lecture me about invading your space, and when he realized I wasn't giving a crap about what he said, he was cool with it. I think living with both Lucille and Kasey is kinda overwhelming him." Camille laughed.

"I can imagine."

"Why don't you go out and have some fun?" Camille suggested.

"Girl, please . . . do you know what happened the last time I went out?" Paige gave her a knowing look.

Camille smiled. "You met Quincy, right?"

"Well, true, but I was talking about the whole robbery at gunpoint thing, remember?" Paige thought about the last time she and Nina were headed to the club, stopping at a convenience store to get some cash from the ATM at the exact moment it was being robbed at gunpoint. Ironically, Quincy was also in the store at the same time, the first time they met.

"Okay, that was kinda messed up. And when I said, 'go out and have some fun,' I meant go and hang out with Quincy. Not everyone can say they have the luxury of a live-in babysitter." Camille shook salt on the popcorn.

"You know you're not a live-in babysitter, Camille. You know I don't even think of you like that." Paige laughed. "Why don't *you* go out and have some fun?"

"Because, unlike you, I don't have a fine man to spend my Friday nights with. You have a life, I don't. You should go have a sleepover of your own." Camille winked and headed up the steps with the bowl.

"I know that's not a booty bag in your hand?" Quincy smiled as he greeted Paige at the door.

"No, it's not. These are my gym clothes."

"Well, this ain't the gym." He laughed.

"I can always put it back in the car," she said, taking a step backward.

"Don't even think about it." He grabbed her and pulled her inside, where she dropped the bag in the middle of the floor and wrapped her arms around him.

He kissed her on the mouth, their tongues tasting one another.

She had wanted him so bad. Things had been tense between them since their lunch date earlier in the week.

Whenever they talked on the phone, it seemed as if he wanted to talk about Marlon and the house situation, which was the last thing she wanted to discuss. She had even found herself making excuses for getting off the phone, something she never had done before. Coming to see him in person was a surefire way to get their relationship back into the right perspective.

She bit his bottom lip, sucking it and reaching under his shirt.

"I thought you had to babysit this weekend?" He panted as he nibbled on her neck.

Paige moaned as his tongue found the sensitive spot on her collarbone. "Camille is at the house with the girls. She told me to come have a sleepover."

"I knew I liked her for a reason," he whispered. He lifted Paige off the floor, and she wrapped her legs around him. She could feel his hardness pressing against her, which made her wet.

He was about to carry her up the steps, when she stopped him. "Wait," she said.

"What?" He looked at her, thinking something was wrong.

She eased off his body and smiled at him. She removed her shirt and skirt, revealing the black lace bra and panty set she wore.

The grin on his face and the bulge in his crotch let her know that he liked it.

She took a few steps upward and then leaned back, reaching up and pulling him toward her.

Understanding exactly what it was she wanted him to do, Quincy wasted no time taking off his shirt and pants. Once again, he kissed her passionately, caressing her hard nipples through the lace.

She licked his shoulders and neck as she opened her legs and placed his fingers there.

He pulled the lace to the side and fingered her wetness.

She groaned. Her fingers made their way to his penis.

In an instant, he shifted his body and tasted her.

Paige grabbed the railing, fearing she would slide down the steps in a fit of ecstasy. Her head rolled back and forth as his tongue went deeper and deeper inside her.

"Q, stop, I can't take it anymore. I want you, please."

Quincy stopped and smiled.

She loved the look of longing in his eyes. Feeling naughtier than usual, Paige turned her back to him, now kneeling on the steps in front of him. She looked back and spread her legs ever so slightly.

"It's like that?"

"If you can handle it." She bit her lip sensually.

Quincy put his arms around her waist and entered her from the back, causing her to gasp.

They rocked back and forth on the stairs for what seemed like hours. When they climaxed together, it was so forceful, that Paige literally screamed.

Panting and sweating, they both collapsed.

"Did I handle it?" He asked, trying to catch his breath.

"It was okay." She laughed and mustered enough energy to rush up the steps to get away from him.

Later that night, after a dinner of Chinese food in bed and more lovemaking, Paige slept in Quincy's arms. The sound of her cell phone ringing on the nightstand caused her to stir.

She looked over and saw that it was Nina calling. "Hello," she said, groggily.

"Paige, it's me."

"I know. What's wrong?"

"I need for you to come and get me."

"Huh?" Paige said, making sure she was hearing Nina right. The clock next to her told her it was well after three in the morning. "Where are you?"

"I'm at the Marriott."

"The what?"

"The Marriott at the Pier—Don't ask any questions, just come get me."

"I'm on my way." Paige looked over at Quincy, who was still sleeping soundly. She eased out of bed and slipped into one of his T-shirts and her jeans. *The things I do for this girl.*

She got into her jeep and drove down the street.

When she arrived at the hotel, Nina was waiting right out front. She tried to see if she could tell if her friend had been harmed in some way, but on the outside, Nina looked fine. She was fully dressed in a pair of slacks and a silk blouse. Her hair and make-up were still in place. She opened the door and got in.

"You all right?"

"I'm fine. Thanks for coming to get me." Nina sighed. She sat back and didn't say anything.

Paige turned the radio up, knowing Nina would talk when she was ready.

Sure enough, Nina asked, "Okay, am I one of these stupid women who seem desperate for a man?"

"Uh, no."

"Then why the hell did I just go through what I went through?"

"What did you just go through?"

"The evening started out great—Craig and I went to dinner, had a few drinks—he made me laugh—went dancing at State Streets, had a few more drinks. I'm telling you, Paige, this was one of the best dates I've been on in years. He's funny and attentive, and I was all over him."

"Okay . . . so then what?"

"He suggests we take a walk down the pier— You know I love romantic shit like that. We go for a walk, he holds my hand, we get to the end of the pier, and he tells me how special I am.

We start kissing—you know I'm horny as hell by now—I haven't had none in months."

"I know." Paige laughed.

"I swear, Paige, out of nowhere, this brother pulls out a room key and points to the Marriott and says, 'You wanna join me on the twenty-fourth floor? It has a great view.' I was shook.

"He takes my hand, we go to the hotel. Not only does he have a room, Paige, but it's a suite, and it's already decked out with rose petals in the Jacuzzi, champagne and strawberries already chilling, R. Kelly playing on the CD player."

"Wow! Like that?"

"Hell yeah, 'like that.' You know me—next thing you know, I'm sitting on the edge of the tub, eating strawberries, and he's in the tub eating me."

Paige couldn't help laughing.

"It's not funny," Nina whined.

"I know. I'm sorry," Paige said, regaining her composure. "Go ahead."

"Check this out—As soon as he lifted me out the tub and placed me on the bed, somebody starts banging on the door. You know I freaked the hell out. I thought it was the police, and I started asking him if he had some warrants!"

"Shut up!" Paige stifled a laugh.

"Paige, why does he tell me, 'Calm down, it was just my wife'? He then tries to get me to go in the bathroom and hide while he got rid of her! He leaves out the room, and I hear them arguing in the hallway. Five minutes later, he comes in and says, 'I took care of it.'"

There was no holding back her laughter now. Paige looked over at her friend. "Nina, come on now, if that happened to me, you would be cracking up too."

Nina didn't crack a smile as she continued with the story. "I told him he was crazy. I got dressed, grabbed my phone, and got out. I called you while I was in the elevator. How about when I got to the lobby, this chick is sitting there talking to the bellhop about, she's waiting on her husband to come out with his mistress—You know I was tripping."

"Is she still there?"

"Hell no, if she was there, do you think I would've been chilling out front waiting on you? It's not meant for me to find a good man." Nina sighed in frustration.

"You have a good man—you just don't want him because he's short," Paige teased.

They pulled up to Nina's townhouse.

"Not funny. Thanks a lot. I don't know what I'd do without you."

"Talk to you later." Paige hugged her best friend.

When she arrived, Quincy was still asleep. She quickly undressed and slipped back into bed as if nothing happened.

The next afternoon, while she was curled in Quincy's arms watching movies, Marlon called. She excused herself and went into the kitchen to take the call.

"Hey, what's up?" he asked.

"Nothing. What's up with you?"

"I just got your message. You said you needed to talk. Anything wrong? Something going on with Myla?"

"No, she's fine. I just wanted to talk, that's all." Paige decided to throw him a bone. "I really want things to be right between us."

"Oh, really? That's all I want, Paige."

She could hear the smugness in his voice.

"There has to be a way that you and I remain friends, Marlon. Our friendship was always the most important part of our relationship, you know that."

"I do know that, Paige. I still love you—that's never gonna change—and I'll always be there for you and Myla, no matter what, I promise."

"I appreciate that, Marlon. That's all I really wanted—to clarify where we stand with each other. The situation between me, Kasey, and your mother has nothing to do with you. And if there's anything that you and I need to deal with, then we can do that."

"I know. That's how it's always been between us."

"Thanks, Marlon. I guess I'll talk to you later."

"All right. If you need anything, you know you can call me. And kiss Myla for me."

"I will."

She knew she had baited him. Now she needed to reel him in, which she planned to do quickly. And his payback was coming hook, line, and sinker.

Chapter 10

"I can't believe how great this place looks." Yaya walked inside. The salon looked better than she ever imagined. The chocolate, teal, and amber décor was warm and inviting. They were all set for the grand opening.

"Lincoln and his crew did a great job," Taryn said. "This is really happening, Yaya."

"Yeah, it is," Yaya told her.

Their dream had come to fruition. In less than twenty-four hours, the doors of After Effex would be open. The invitations to the grand opening reception had been sent, and they were putting the final touches on the decorations.

Monya was placing balloons strategically, while Taryn and Yaya were putting key chains and Carol's Daughter samples into goodie bags.

"Did you get the shirts, Monya?" Taryn asked.

Monya picked up the special-order baby T's the girls had finally agreed upon. "Right here. So, it's these? Black jeans and what shoes?"

"All-black Jordans," Taryn anwered.

"I don't want to wear sneakers," Yaya complained again.

They had been going back and forth about this for days, and she was still trying to convince them to wear something else.

"It's not up for discussion. I suggest you run by the mall and pick you up a pair when you leave here. Better yet, run next door and see if Twan can hook you up with a pair out his trunk," Taryn told her. "We agreed. Now, that's it. We want people to feel comfortable when they come in here."

"If we had opened downtown like we wanted, they would feel comfortable," Yaya murmured.

"Here we go again," Monya groaned.

"Let it go, Yaya," Taryn told her. "Did you call the caterer and give her a final count?"

"Yes, I did. They'll be here at nine in the morning to set up."

"Taryn, which box did you put the extra towels in?" Monya called from the back.

"Hold on. I'll come and get them. I hope she hasn't rearranged anything."

Yaya placed the filled bags neatly behind the counter. "Better hide these. I know this place is gonna have some chickenheads looking for freebies tomorrow, and these are for paying customers only."

The sound of the door chimes let her know someone had come in.

"Wow! This place looks great."

Yaya turned around to make sure her ears weren't deceiving her. "Jason!"

"This is nice." He walked over and hugged her tight.

Yaya's mood changed instantly. Her heart began fluttering, and she was smiling from the inside out.

"You like it? Really?" She looked at him to make sure he approved.

"It's beautiful, Yaya. I'm so proud of you." He smiled. "I can't believe you really did it."

"What's up, Jason," Taryn greeted him.

Monya did the same. "Hi, Jason."

"Ladies, you really outdid yourselves. I can't believe how good it looks in here. I got my invitation in the mail. So tomorrow's the big day, huh?"

"Yep." Yaya nodded. "You're gonna stop by, right?"

"Of course, I am, Ya. You know I wouldn't miss it. This is your dream." He touched her hand softly, and tingles ran up her arm.

The door chimed again.

"Yo, *J*, I thought you were only gonna be in here in a minute."

The joy that Yaya was feeling left her body and was replaced by disgust. Impeccably dressed in a Brooks Brothers suit and a pair of Steve Madden loafers, Travis Thorne strolled in and gave Yaya a fake smile. "Hey, Yaya. Nice spot."

"Thanks." Yaya gave him a dirty look. She was still pissed about his letting that hag drive her car.

He walked over and stood in front of Taryn, staring at her cleavage as he normally did. "Two tons of fun, nice to see you again."

"Always an asshole, huh, Travis." Taryn folded her arms across her chest.

"Why it's gotta be like that, Taryn? I thought we were better than that."

"You thought wrong, Travis." She brushed by him.

"I swear, if I dated big girls, Taryn, you and I would probably be married by now. And I see you even got pretty Monya in on your little nail shop." He grinned.

Monya rolled her eyes at him.

"Yo, you ready to roll?"

"Give me a sec, Trav," Jason told him; "I'll be right there."

"He's such a jerk. I can't believe you really hang with him," Yaya said after he left.

"Just ignore him. Is there somewhere we can talk?"

"Sure. We can go back in my office." She led him to the small office she was proud to call her own. It was just large enough to hold a desk for her computer and two chairs. "It's not all that big, but it works for me."

"It's nice. Check out the picture—Is that a Cathy Parker?" He peered at the painting hanging on the wall.

"Yeah, it's *The French Connection*." Yaya was pleased he noticed the original painting by one of her favorite artists. The framed picture of a man and a woman about to French-kiss was erotic, yet tasteful.

"Nice touch." He nodded.

"I miss you."

"I miss you too." He reached out and took her hand. "I'm so proud of you."

"I couldn't have done any of this without you, Jason. You were the one who told me to make my plan and work my plan, remember?" She stepped closer to him.

"But you were the one who did it, and very well, I might add." He touched her cheek. "Pretty Girl."

She closed her eyes and savored the moment. *Pretty Girl* was the name he had given her when they first met. He said she looked like an innocent Janet Jackson, during her years on *Fame* when Janet was a pretty girl and not a nasty girl. She even had Janet's body; he always told her she was his fantasy woman.

"Jason—"

His cell phone ringing interrupted her. He took it out of his pocket, "A'ight, man, I'm coming out now." He closed it and told her, "I gotta run, but I will see you tomorrow at the reception. And tomorrow night, we'll have a celebration of our own, a'ight?"

"A'ight."

He put his hand under her chin and tilted her head up.

She closed her eyes, as his lips met hers and kissed her softly.

"Bye, Pretty Girl," he said and walked out.

Finally, things were looking better. Jason had come to his senses, and things were back to normal. She couldn't wait until tomorrow night. Having him come and tell her how proud he was of her validated Yaya's feeling of accomplishment. She knew that opening the salon was a risk, but having his vote of approval gave her just the vote of confidence she needed. She floated out of her office and back into the salon.

"I take it the break is over?" Taryn asked.

"Break is over." She smiled.

"Thank God . . . because I couldn't take another day of your moping." Taryn walked over and gave her a hug.

"Okay. Break open a bottle of champagne. Forget waiting 'til tomorrow!" Yaya declared.

"Now that's what I'm talking 'bout." Monya ran to the back and returned with a bottle and three plastic glasses.

"Where is the music? We 'bout to get this party started *now*!"

The boom box was now replaced by an iPod, which they docked on a surround-sound station. She scrolled through the hand-held device until she found Janet Jackson and hit the title, "You Want This." She turned the volume all the way up, and the girls began dancing.

They were jamming, when the door opened and Jarrod walked in.

"What the hell are y'all doing over here? Turn that shit down some!" He yelled.

The three of them looked at him and then each other. They danced in a circle around him closer and closer until he was sandwiched between them. Unable to resist, he began dancing and gyrating along with them.

Moments later, Quincy walked in. "What in the world?"

"They jumped me, man. Wasn't nothing I could do," Jarrod said, without missing a beat.

"Yeah, right!" Quincy said.

"I'm serious." Jarrod shrugged. "Yo, show him what y'all working with."

The three ladies eased away from Jarrod and circled Quincy. They were so enticing that he found himself dancing, like Jarrod, as well.

A few other guys came over to see what was going on, and before they knew it, a full-blown party had ensued.

"See why I didn't want a walkthrough doorway." Yaya laughed in her brother's ear.

The next morning, decked out in their black After Effex baby T's, black jeans, and sure enough, all black Air Jordans, courtesy of Twan, who had so much fun at the pre-grand opening party, he gave them each a pair.

Qianna, Taryn and Monya cut the ribbon and opened the doors of After Effex Salon. They had taken care of every little detail, and everything went smoothly: The caterers arrived on time, and the food was delicious; the photographers took shots of everyone and everything; the deejay played the right music at just the right time.

Family, friends, and colleagues all came out to show their support. From top fashion models in the industry to brides whose faces Yaya or Taryn had done on their wedding day, it seemed as if everyone who got an invitation showed up.

Quincy had gone all out, calling in all sorts of favors and taking care of most of the marketing for the girls. The radio station did a live broadcast, and even the newspaper did an interview with them.

Monya and Taryn did nails nonstop. Yaya filled the role of hostess, make-up artist and receptionist at the same time; she was in her element.

"Yo, Yaya, come here for a moment," Quincy called from the front of the salon.

She walked over to see him standing beside a beautiful woman with short, wavy hair and the cutest little girl. "What's up, Q?"

She noticed that he was holding the woman's hand. No doubt, the woman's looks were striking, but she was different from any woman she had ever seen her brother with. Quincy always went for tall, dark, slim women. Paige was barely five foot five, almond-colored, and clearly a size twelve.

"Yaya, this is Paige. Paige, this is my sister, Yaya." He beamed.

"Nice to meet you. You can call me Yaya." She held her hand out to Paige. "And who is this pretty woman?"

"That is Ms. Myla." Quincy reached over and rubbed the little girl's head. "Paige's daughter."

Yaya was shocked by her brother's behavior. Quincy rarely, if ever, showed any public displays of affection. To see him openly holding Paige's hand and showing attention to her daughter let Yaya know that her brother had to be feeling something for this woman. But he hadn't even talked to her about Paige.

Usually, Quincy would allow Yaya to meet girls before he dated them on the regular, let alone become involved with them on a serious level. Most women often looked forward to meeting her, when he mentioned he had a sister; if they didn't, they had to be hiding something.

"I have heard so much about you," Paige told her. "Your brother is so proud of you. You're all he ever talks about."

"All good things, I hope." Yaya smiled. She checked Paige out. *He hasn't said anything about you. And a daughter?—Quincy doesn't do baby mamas—he says they have too much bag-gage—What is up with this?*

"You know I never have anything bad to say about you, sis. I'm gonna show Paige and Myla around the place."

"Your salon is beautiful," Paige said. "Let me know if there's anything I can do to help. I know it's going to be a big success."

Something in the way she said it made Yaya feel warm inside. It was as if Paige believed in her without even knowing her.

She still remained hesitant about liking her. She had been used plenty of times before by females trying to get in good with Quincy—they thought that if they could win her over, it was a surefire way to become the future Mrs. Quincy Westbrooke. And having a child already probably gave Paige even stronger ulterior motives for dating Quincy.

If Paige thought for one moment that she was going to get her hooks in her brother and poof, instant family, she was mistaken. She made a mental note to have a heart-to-heart with her brother and see what was up with that.

A few hours later, Yaya checked her watch and saw that it was after four and Jason hadn't made it. The salon was crowded, and people were still coming in. She called his cell phone and didn't get an answer.

"What's going on, people?" Lincoln gave a hearty greeting as he walked in the door.

"Yo, Linc, my man, you hooked this place up!" Quincy walked over and gave him a hug.

"What's up, Lincoln?" Taryn, hard at work on Paige's nails, paused long enough to check herself in the mirror to make sure she was looking tight as ever.

Lincoln walked over, leaned and gave her a kiss on the cheek.

She looked over at Yaya and winked.

"Congratulations."

Yaya looked up and stared right into the eyes of Fitzgerald.

He was smiling at her.

She couldn't help smiling back. "Thank you. Where's Carter? He better not be out there in my parking lot unattended."

"Ha! It's *Carver*, and no, he's not here to terrorize you today. I left him home, seeing that it was the grand opening and all; I didn't want to scare off any potential new customers."

"Thanks. You're so considerate," she told him.

"I see your gala is a success. Linc told me you were worried people wouldn't wanna come to the hood when you opened."

Yaya wondered what else Lincoln felt the need to share with Fitz. "That's not true. Well, not exactly true."

"Yeah, right." He laughed.

She tried not to notice how attractive he was in his jeans and long white T-shirt. His dreads were hanging today, and he had on a pair of what looked to be brand-new white Nike's.

"Well, I just wanted to say congratulations."

"Thank you, Fitz. Listen, hang out for a while, grab a plate, get a manicure. I can even hook those brows up if you want."

"My brows?—I don't think so." He touched them.

She stared into his strong grey eyes.

"But I will get a plate."

"Enjoy. Here's a coupon in case you want that manicure, though."

She passed him the small slip of paper, which entitled him to three dollars off.

He walked over to the buffet table and began talking with Quincy and Lincoln.

She felt someone staring at her and checked to see where it was coming from. Taryn and Monya both were smiling as if they had discovered some deep, dark secret she was hiding from them and there was nothing she could do about it.

"What? Get back to work," she snapped at them, and they giggled.

For the hundredth time that day, Yaya looked around to see if Jason had slipped by her and she missed his coming through the door. She was again disappointed to see he wasn't there.

"Are you all booked for today?" someone asked. Two women were standing at the receptionist's area.

"I'm sorry. Yeah, we are." Yaya looked down at the book and saw that they were almost booked for the next two weeks. Yaya was tickled to death.

"My girlfriend told me to get here early, but somebody held me up at the mall." The woman elbowed the young-looking girl standing beside her.

"I said, 'Sorry,'" the younger girl said. "You know I was filling out applications."

Feeling sorry for the women, Yaya agreed to squeeze them in on Monday and even doubled their coupon.

"'Bout time you got here." Paige walked over to them.

"They're booked up," the woman said. "Camille here decided to fill out a million applications."

"I figured since we were already at the mall, I would go ahead and apply for some jobs." Camille shrugged.

"Yaya, this is my best friend Nina, and my sister-in-law, Camille," Paige said, introducing them.

"Oh, okay. Welcome." Yaya smiled. "Yeah, there's no way we can take anyone else today. But I promised to hook them up on Monday."

"I know you will." Paige smiled. She held up her perfectly manicured hands—"Check it out."

"Niiiiiceeeeee." Nina admired her nails. "And look at that. Can I get a serving of him?—super-size, please?"

"Girl, make mine a double," Camille added. "I just wanna run my fingers through his dreads."

Yaya looked to see they were talking about Fitzgerald.

"Camille, cut it out. Nina, stop encouraging her," Paige hissed as they walked off.

Yaya laughed, amused by their reaction.

It was well after nine when the last customer left the salon. The girls were exhausted.

"It's over!" Monya said, locking the door.

"I can't believe we did it. We are officially in business." Taryn collapsed on the sofa of the waiting area.

"I just wanna go home and get in my bed." Monya fell into the matching chair next to Taryn.

"What about our plans to go have a drink?" Taryn asked.

"I'm too tired," Monya told her.

"But I told Lincoln and Jarrod we were coming over to State Streets," Taryn replied. "We've gotta go; I'm tired too. Come on."

"Fine." Monya sighed. "But just one drink."

"I just don't want to stand them up. You ready, Ya? What's wrong?—You been quiet for a while now."

Yaya shook her head. "Nothing. Just tired." She stretched her arms.

Truth is, she was irritated. Today had come and gone, and Jason never showed up. He hadn't even called. The most important day of her life, and he wasn't there.

Monya sat up. "I guess we need to change before we go to the club, huh?"

"No doubt. You know we can't step in there with jeans and sneakers on . . . although the shirts would make great advertisement." Taryn looked down at her shirt. "Like walking billboards."

"How come your words look bigger than mine?" Monya looked at hers, pointing out the difference.

"It's not the size of the words, boo-boo, it's the size of the billboard." Taryn laughed. "Oh, I almost forgot. I have something for you both." She walked into the back and returned with two small, black gift bags and gave one to Yaya and Monya.

"What is this?" Yaya reached inside and took out a small black, velvet box. She slowly opened it and gasped as she saw the small diamond-clustered pendant with the words *After Effex*. Tears came to her eyes. "Oh, *T*, it's beautiful."

"Awwww, I love it." Monya lifted hers out of the box. "Now I feel bad because I didn't get you anything."

"Don't worry, we'll have plenty of other occasions for you to buy me gifts," Taryn said. "Besides, you know I bought myself one. It's just my way of saying, 'I love you and know that we're all in this together.'"

"Well, I just want to say thank you to you both. Even though this is *your* salon because it was *your* idea, and *you* all put the money up. You both make my feel like I'm just as important," Monya told her.

'You are just as important, Monya." Yaya walked over and hugged her. "It's not about the money; you worked just as hard as we did in making this happen."

Taryn joined in. "Hell, you worked harder than Yaya." She reached into Monya's hand, taking the necklace out the box and putting it around the girl's neck.

Monya did the same for Yaya, and Yaya for Taryn. It had been an emotional day for all of them, and there was no way to stop the tears from falling.

"Okay, if we don't get outta here, there's no way I'm gonna make it to the club." Monya wiped her eyes. "You gonna scoop me up, *T*? You know my truck is on *E*."

"Yeah, I know. Yaya, you want me to pick you up?"

"I can meet you there." Yaya really didn't feel up to partying, but she didn't want to spoil the mood. "Let's say, an hour?"

"Cool. Call when you leave your house." Taryn nodded. "Perk up, Yaya—you know if Lincoln is there, Fitzgerald probably will be there too."

"I don't care." Yaya looked at her like she was crazy.

"Maybe you need to, especially since Jason wasn't in your face today—Fitz was," Monya told her. "I wonder if they have another brother for me? You know good things always come in threes."

"Lincoln's never mentioned another brother." Taryn shrugged.

"Who knows, they may have a cousin named *Washington* for you," Yaya joked.

"That's not funny, Yaya," Taryn snapped as they walked out of the building.

"Yes, it was." Yaya locked the door behind them.

She didn't understand why they kept bringing up Fitzgerald, when they knew she had just gotten back with Jason. Never mind the fact that he was not her type.

Hell, he drives a Honda Accord station wagon, for God's sake. Taryn knows that I don't roll like that.

Chapter 11

"Baby, do you know anything about the Benz for sale outside Titus' shop?" Paige asked Quincy as she set paper products on her picnic table.

It was a nice Saturday afternoon, and they'd decided to cook out in her backyard. They had invited her mother, along with Aunt Connie, Meeko and her family, Nina and Jade, and a few other family members, including her father.

"Yeah, it's nice, huh? That fool put it up for sale knowing he had to go out of town. Why?—you know somebody interested in it." Quincy looked up from the grill.

"Maybe. You know how much he wants for it?"

"Depends on who's interested."

"You act like you got some type of pull or something." She walked over and wrapped her arms around his waist. She buried her head in his shoulder and inhaled his scent. She loved touching him. It was as if she was drawn to him. It was love, no doubt about it.

"I do. I mean, after all, the man is my best friend."

"So what does a sister have to do to get you to talk to your best friend and get me a good deal?"

He turned around and kissed her. "I'm sure you can think of something."

"Uh, not over the food, thanks." Camille came out, carrying a tray of meat to put on the grill.

"Be quiet before I burn your steak, youngster," Quincy warned.

"Steak? She doesn't get a steak," Paige said; "only working people get steak."

"That's not fair," Camille said. "You know I've been looking for a job."

"Yeah—at the mall." Paige laughed. "You just want to work where you can meet men and get a discount."

"I'm just trying to make the most of my place of employment. You can't blame me for being resourceful."

Quincy nodded. "That's true."

"You know what—I just had the bomb idea"— Camille snapped her fingers. "You should call Yaya and hook me up with a job at the salon. They are mad busy and look like they can use the help."

Quincy turned the meat over. "Oh, really? Are you a nail tech?"

"No."

"A make-up artist?"

"No."

"Then why should they hire you?" He looked over at Paige to see her reaction.

She looked at Camille and waited for her answer.

"Because . . . I would make the bomb receptionist, that's why. I told you I'm the most resourceful person in the world, so I know how to make the most of their time. Not only that, but there's no one in the city that knows more about Carol's Daughter than me. They are sitting on a gold mine and don't even know it. They aren't even marketing that to the customers like they should. I worked at Foot Locker last summer, so I have retail experience and I know how to sell."

Camille said it all in one breath. "So can you hook me up?"

"Wow! I'm impressed," Quincy said.

"I trained her well." Paige walked and put her arm around Camille. "So can you hook us up?"

"'Us?'" Camille asked.

"Shut up and let me handle this," Paige hissed.

"I guess I can see what I can do for both of you." He sighed.

"Thanks, baby." Paige grinned and winked at Camille.

"Yeah, thanks, baby," Camille mocked.

Before long, their guests arrived, and the cookout was in full swing. It was the first time in a long time that her family had gotten together without any tension, chaos, and more importantly, drama. Even her estranged mother and father were sitting back and seemed to be enjoying each other, which was unusual for them.

"I am having so much fun," Meeko told Paige as she passed her the baby.

Paige's bedroom gave her the privacy she needed to feed Isaiah; a chance to cool off. "I'm glad you are. Seems like everyone is." Paige cradled Isaiah into her arms. He was so tiny and adorable. It made her think of her own son, who passed away moments after being born. She stared at his small face and smiled. "You are so precious."

"Don't play with me, Paige—you know my baby is not *Precious*!"

"I meant that in a good way!" Paige laughed. "Isaiah is the most beautiful baby boy ever born—next to Myles, that is."

"I'll take that." Meeko smiled. "You know, we were so worried about your reaction to the baby. Now I feel stupid because we had nothing to worry about."

"You're kidding, right?" Paige frowned. "How did you think I was going to react?"

"I don't know. Aunt Gayle said she wouldn't be surprised if you stopped hanging around me, and we would grow apart because maybe, in a sense, you would be jealous," Meeko confessed. "I couldn't really see that happening, but I was concerned that Isaiah would make you think about Myles."

"Meeko, I think about Myles every day. He was my son, and I miss him. But I would never begrudge you because you had a baby. That's crazy." Paige couldn't believe her aunt would say such a thing about her. "Was I jealous when you got married?"

"No."

"I was happy for you, the same way I am now. Now if Aunt Gayle wants to go there, then you should point out who did complain the entire time we planned your wedding. They didn't like the dresses, they didn't like the colors, they didn't like this, they didn't like that."

"Now that was her and Celeste." Meeko laughed.

"You're damn right, it was them."

The baby began whining, and Paige placed the pacifier in his mouth.

"Where are they anyway?" Meeko asked. "Don't tell me you didn't invite them."

Paige shot a knowing glance at her cousin. "You know I didn't want to, but Mama called and told them about it, saying they were family and still had to be a part of it. Celeste already had plans with a friend, thank God. And Aunt Gayle said she wasn't up to coming."

"Out of town?" Meeko smirked. "That girl ain't nowhere, but riding that bus to see Cofie in the pen—she ain't got no friends."

"'Cofie?—I know she ain't still messing with that two-time loser, come on now," Paige said.

Before she supposedly started her imaginary relationship with Quincy, Celeste's man was Cofie. She had met him while he was locked up—he'd accidentally called their house collect, and she accepted the charges. The two exchanged letters and phone calls for over a year, and by the time he made parole, Celeste swore she was in love, and they were engaged.

Cofie put the wedding on hold as soon as he got out, saying he wanted to save some money because he wanted a big wedding. The problem was that five months later, he was caught driving without a license and carrying a concealed weapon. He went back to jail, and according to Celeste, she rarely spoke to him.

"Still talks to him every day. Aunt Gayle called Mama to borrow money because they phone bill was over six hundred dollars last month and that mug was about to get cut off."

"I know your mama ain't give it to her."

"No. Mama told her, 'Maybe it needed to be cut off, since Celeste didn't have sense enough to just say no when he called collect.'"

"That's ridiculous," Paige said.

"Mom!" Myla screamed. "Come down here quick!"

From the tone of her voice, Paige knew something was wrong. She handed Meeko the baby and rushed down the steps.

"Myla, what's wrong?"

Myla was standing in front of the door, looking as if she had seen a ghost.

Paige moved her daughter to the side to see what had caused her to scream her name. Standing at the door was Celeste.

"Oh, what's up, Celeste?" Paige was still confused by her daughter's reaction to her cousin. "Myla, why did you call me like that? And why didn't you let her in?"

"I don't know what her problem is," Celeste said nastily, rolling her eyes at the little girl. "I was about to feel unwelcome."

Still confused, Paige started unlocking the screen door. "No, you can come in, Celeste."

"Thanks. Oh and I hope you don't mind—I brought a guest."

There was something in the way that Celeste said it that made Paige stop dead in her tracks. Her hand fell to her side, and the door remained shut.

"I think you know Kasey; she used to live down the street from you."

"Hello, Paige." Kasey stared at Paige.

"Celeste, you have lost your damn mind. Myla, go outside and stay—don't come back in here do you understand?"

"Yes." Myla didn't hesitate running out the back door.

"Oh, hell naw." Meeko got to the bottom of the steps and saw who was on the other side of the door. "Celeste, are you crazy? I know you didn't bring that girl to Paige's house."

"Whatever, Meeko. Aunt Jackie called me last week and said I was invited to Paige's house for a cookout. I asked her, 'Could I bring a friend?' and her words to me were, 'The more, the merrier.' So I'm here." Celeste smirked.

Paige continued to stare at both women, whom she hated. The anger inside her was so great that she began sweating, even in the cold air that was blasting through the vent. Her heart began pounding, and she couldn't bring herself to blink for fear that in that split second, Celeste and Kasey may come to their senses and get the hell away from her doorstep, and she wouldn't get the chance to whup their asses.

"Uh, we're waiting." Celeste shrugged.

"Leave, Celeste, now. You know this ain't right." Meeko stepped beside Paige.

"And her dating Quincy is right, even though she knew I had feelings for him?" Celeste rolled her neck.

"Girl, please," Kasey spat. "I keep telling you she ain't thinking about Quincy—she's too busy trying to get back with Marlon, knowing I'm his wife and having his baby!"

"I think you both need to leave," Quincy's voice said.

Paige could feel him behind her, but she didn't move. She continued to stare at them.

"Well, well, well . . . if it isn't the man himself. What's up, Quincy?" Celeste had the nerve to smile.

"Celeste Denise Harper, I can't believe you," Paige's mother said.

"Hey, Aunt Jackie. Paige won't let us in. I told her you said I could bring a friend." Celeste tried to sound innocent.

"You're wrong, Celeste," she said.

"So is your beloved daughter, Aunt Jackie, but I don't wanna go there. We just wanted to come through and get a plate."

"Well, I wanna go there," Kasey said. "Can you tell me why you're calling my husband's cell phone all times of the night?"

"What?" Meeko asked; Paige didn't have to.

"She's calling Marlon and talking to him on his cell phone every night, sometimes two or three times a night."

"Kasey, shut the hell up and just leave. You know she don't want Marlon's triflin' ass. Sorry, Aunt Jackie," Meeko said. "I don't mean any disrespect."

"That's okay."

"I don't have to lie—the proof is right here in black and white." Kasey reached into her bag and pulled out a thick wad of folded papers—"Let's see, May 3rd, 11:18 p.m., 7394898, May 4th, 12:19 p.m., May 5th, 11:36 p.m—Isn't that your telephone number?"

"So what if it is?" Quincy shrugged. "That's her daughter's father. He may be talking to Myla."

"Bullshit! You know at eleven o'clock at night Myla is in the bed. Don't be stupid, Quincy. She ain't calling you at eleven at night. She's calling Marlon, blowing his phone up." Celeste smirked.

Paige still remained silent, not moving.

"Say something, Paige—Everyone thinks you're this perfect person who can do no wrong. I guess it's true what they say—what's done in the dark . . ."

Kasey said. "At least be woman enough to admit you're trying to get back with Marlon."

"She ain't thinking about Marlon," Meeko said.

"Then why is she calling him?" Kasey yelled.

"She ain't calling him." Quincy raised his voice.

"Then who is?" Kasey demanded.

"I am, bitch. He is my brother! Now please leave!"

Everyone except Paige turned to see Camille standing with her arms folded.

A smile spread across Paige's face. She took a step back and slammed the door and locked it.

"Anybody ready for dessert?"

Chapter 12

Yaya answered the ringing telephone. "Thanks for calling After Effex, where before and after are never the same."

She was wearing herself thin, and it was taking its toll on her. They had been open for almost two weeks and had more business than they could handle. All three of them were working twelve-hour days, and she was exhausted.

She blinked several times and tried to focus on what the woman on the other end was saying.

"Monya has a 3:30 slot available next Wednesday, is that okay? Okay, Tam, I'll put you down, and thanks for calling."

As soon as she hung the phone up, it began ringing again.

"We need to hire a secretary," Taryn said as she put the final touches on a pedicure she was doing.

"I know. I was trying to hold out until next month." Yaya sighed.

"That's not gonna work, Yaya. You have to do faces for the hair book shoot next week. Who's gonna answer the phones?"

"I almost forgot about that. I need to write it in the book, huh?" Yaya flipped the page.

"Yaya, you didn't right it down? You gotta get better, girl."

Yaya stretched her neck. She didn't feel well and wanted to go home and get in her bed. "I will, I promise."

The door opened, and in walked two heavyset women.

"Hello, we have a one-thirty nail appointment," the first one said. She was brown-skinned with glasses, plainly dressed in sneakers, sweats, and an oversized T-shirt. The second woman was looking around as if she had never been in a nail salon before. She was caramel-colored with light eyes and had the biggest lips Yaya had ever seen.

They were exactly the clientele Yaya did *not* want to attract. *Here come the hoodrats.* She glanced up to see Taryn giving her a warning look.

Yaya quickly told them, "Have a seat. Someone will be with you in a few moments."

"Thanks."

The dark woman smiled, and they took a seat in the waiting area.

"This is a really nice place. As soon as I heard this was Quincy's sister's place, I had to come."

"You know Quincy? I'm his sister."

"Oh, you must be Qianna. I've heard so much about you."

"What's your name?" Yaya asked her.

"Oh, I'm Celeste," she said, in a way that made Yaya think she thought it should mean something, which it didn't.

"Nice to meet you. Taryn will take care of you as soon as she's finished over there, and Monya, our other nail technician, will be right in. She just stepped out to grab some lunch."

"You don't do nails?" Celeste seemed disappointed.

"No, make-up is my specialty."

"All right now. I may need to get in your chair before I leave." The second woman grinned, showing Yaya her big teeth.

I ain't a miracle worker. "I can hook you up."

Monya waltzed in carrying a large bag of food. "Lunch has arrived."

"Don't start eating," Yaya told her; "you have a client."

"I do? I didn't see anything on the books."

"We called last week," Celeste said.

Yaya looked back at the book. "Ooops, I put you down for tomorrow, my bad!"

"Yaya!" Taryn and Monya said at the same time.

"Okay, I got it."

"Yaya can take care of your next appointment for you, I think," Taryn told her client as she left.

A few moments later she announced, "You ladies can come on over."

The two women walked over to the pedicure area and sat in the large princess chairs.

"So how do you know Quincy?" Taryn asked as she began filling the foot tubs with warm water.

"Oh, we went out a couple of times." Celeste grinned. "That's my boo."

Yeah, right. I don't think so. You look like Al Roker's sister. Yaya prayed she wouldn't laugh out loud.

"Really?" Taryn said. "I heard that."

"Yeah, I love me some *Q*," Celeste said. "He's a good man. And we all know a good man is hard to find."

"Too bad he's taken now." Monya took a seat in front of Celeste's friend. "How'd you let that happen?"

"He ain't taken." Celeste laughed.

"I'm sorry, Celeste, but he is. I met his girl-friend the other day." Yaya nodded. She didn't want the woman getting her hopes up thinking that she even had a chance with her brother.

"Who? Paige? Please . . . She's about to be old news. Quincy won't be with her long." Celeste sat up.

"Hold please." Yaya put the customer on hold, interested in what Celeste had to say. "Why not?"

"She's a skank, that's why. And Quincy's gonna find out about it," Celeste told her.

"We must not be talking about the same girl. This girl is kinda short, curvy, short hair, gorgeous," Yaya said. "She's classy. Had a pretty little girl with her."

"I wouldn't say she was gorgeous, but she is short and dumpy," the other woman told her. "The little girl is her brat, Myla."

"Sounds like someone is hating," Taryn teased. "Paige seemed really nice when she came in. She's also been sending business our way. Her best friend and her sister-in-law have come in."

"'Sister-in-law'? Paige has never been married, and she is an only child." Celeste guffawed.

"No, I'm sure this girl is her sister-in-law. She even introduced her as her sister. What's her name, Monya—the smart, pretty girl who told us about the new summer line coming out from Carol's Daughter?"

"Oh, Camille. She was crazy." Monya laughed. "Yeah, she did say she was Paige's sister-in-law."

"Camille isn't Paige's sister-in-law." Celeste frowned. "She's Myla's aunt. That's Paige's baby daddy's sister who lives with them."

Yaya's eyes widened. She looked to Taryn and Monya who, oddly enough, were engrossed in the pedicures.

"I'm telling you, Paige is no good, and your brother deserves better. I keep trying to tell him, but she got him so wide-open that he can't even hear me. I may joke around about him being my boo and all, but he's my friend and I don't wanna see him used or hurt."

"I know that's right." Her friend nodded. "Paige got a lot of shit with her. Your brother needs to watch out."

The phone began ringing again, and Yaya began taking calls again. She tried to concentrate but found herself straining to hear what Celeste was saying as she talked to Monya and Taryn.

"Thank you so much," Celeste said when they had finished. "I can't wait to come back again."

"I'm glad you liked it," Yaya said as she hung the phone up for the hundredth time since they had arrived.

"I'm not trying to be messy, but I meant what I said—I care about your brother, and he deserves better." Celeste paid Yaya. "Maybe you can talk some sense into him."

Yaya gave her back some change. "I'll keep that in mind."

"I heard you said you need a receptionist. I'm looking for a second job myself because I really need the money. I can bring a lot to your salon and help you out a lot." Celeste looked at Yaya intensely.

Yaya read between the lines and smiled. "When can you start?"

"Yaya, I don't know about this. I don't think hiring that girl was a smart idea," Taryn said.

"You're the one that was stressing about a receptionist. What's the big deal?—She said she can start tomorrow."

"I don't like her," Monya said. "And how could you just hire her without even talking to us?"

Yaya began rubbing her temples. They were making her head hurt. And what made Monya think she had the right to question who she hired anyway? She was an employee, not the employer.

"What was I supposed to say? She was standing right there asking for the job?" Yaya snapped.

"How about, 'Let me get back with you,' or 'I'll give you a call'?" Taryn answered.

"My head is hurting." Yaya lay her head on the desk.

"Join the club." Monya walked over to the bag she laid down earlier and took out a Styrofoam plate. "Dang, I didn't even have time to eat today."

"What is that?" Taryn asked.

"Stewed chicken, peas and rice, and some macaroni and cheese. Your head is probably hurting because you're hungry—You want some? I'm 'bout to heat it up and throw down."

"I do. Put me some on a plate."

"No, thanks," Yaya answered.

"Suit yourself." Taryn walked into the back.

"A'ight, Yaya, what's going on with you? I know you're tired, but I also know something else is wrong." Taryn walked over and leaned on the desk where Yaya's head was still buried. "You're not pregnant, are you?"

"What? Since when is a headache a pregnancy symptom?" Yaya sat up and gave her a mean look. "You know I ain't pregnant, fool. Hell, that would require sex."

"You're not pregnant, are you?" Taryn asked again, her eyes wide.

"No, Taryn, I'm not pregnant."

"I know you haven't said anything, but are you and Jason still working things out?"

"Yeah, we're good," she lied.

Yaya didn't want to admit to her friends that she and Jason were no closer than the day he decided to take a break. Lying about their relationship was easier than defending the fact that she still loved him.

"He just wants to take things a little slow, you know, give each other a little space. We both have a lot going on right now."

"That's a good thing, Yaya. You've been with Jason for three years, while he's made his moves and climbed the corporate ladder. Now it's time to do you. Take advantage of this time and enjoy your life for a change."

"I've always done me," Yaya said.

"No, you did what Jason allowed you to do," Taryn told her. "How many times did you have to cut out early on a job because you had to meet Jason to have dinner with one of his clients? Or the times you turned down jobs because Jason said you were traveling too much. I don't even want to mention the parties you missed out on because Jason didn't want to come with you. You think we don't know why you didn't show up at State Street the night of the grand opening? We know you were with Jason."

She was busted. When she arrived home opening night, Jason was waiting for her, glass of wine in hand, ready to sex her the way she had been craving. As soon as he finished, he was gone.

Yaya sat silently listening to Taryn. Most of what her best friend was saying was true. She had compromised a lot for her relationship with Jason, but she had gained a lot too. That's what love's about—give and take.

Taryn was right about her failure to appear at State Street. She was with Jason; but she refused to admit it.

Monya walked in and passed Taryn her plate.

The enticing aroma caused Yaya's stomach to growl. She looked at her friends stirring their food. Unable to resist any longer, she told Monya, "Let me taste that."

"I asked you, 'Did you want some'?" Monya passed her a forkful of chicken and rice.

Yaya tasted the food. "Wow! This is the bomb. Where did you get it from?"

"Someplace Jarrod told me about called Ochie's," Monya said, taking her fork back.

"In the Bottoms?" Yaya gasped, thinking about the worst, most crime-ridden part of the city she'd never dare go.

"Yeah." Monya laughed.

"You went to the Bottoms? By yourself? Are you crazy?" Yaya's jaw dropped.

"Yaya, please . . . there's nothing wrong with the Bottoms." Taryn shook her head. "Stop trippin'."

"I ain't trippin'." Yaya reached for Monya's fork again. "I just can't believe you went by yourself."

"I asked you, 'Did you want some'?" Monya passed her the plate.

There was a loud rumbling outside the shop, and they all looked out the window. Yaya instantly recognized the large purple-and-white bike that was pulling in front.

"Who let the dogs out?" Taryn shouted as the door opened and Quincy walked in.

He removed his helmet and placed it on the sofa.

"Excuse me, the sign says no loitering," Yaya announced. "This establishment is for paying customers only. If you're trying to loiter for free, you need to go next door to Q-Masters."

"How about this building is for paying tenants only." Quincy raised his eyebrows at her.

"What's up, Quincy? Come on in. Have a seat. Take a load off." She smiled at him.

"I thought you would change your song." He walked over and hugged her. "How's business?"

"Almost more than we can handle," Taryn told him. "I love it."

"Jarrod told me it stays packed in here." Quincy looked around. "Since it's like that, maybe I should charge—"

Yaya stopped him. "Don't even try it."

"I'm glad things are going well for you." Quincy looked at the plate in front of her. "That looks good. Where did you get it?"

"Ochie's," she told him.

"Ochie's?" Quincy looked shocked. "You went to Ochie's?"

"No, Monya went." She rolled her eyes. "And what if I said I did?"

"You'd be lying," he told her. "So have you hired a secretary yet? I know someone looking for a job."

"Who?" Taryn spoke up.

"Paige's sister-in-law, Camille, you met her. She came in last week with Paige's best friend, Nina," he said.

Yaya saw the reflection of Monya and Taryn in the mirror. She turned and gave them a threatening look. "Sorry, we just hired someone this afternoon."

"Really? That was quick. Well, if you need anyone else, or the person doesn't work out, let me know. The girl is smart, and I think she'd do a good job."

She ignored Taryn's shaking head and told him, "I will. Hey, *Q*, have you talked to Titus? I've been trying to reach him and I can't. I know he's outta town. When is he coming back?"

"He should be back next week. I'll tell him you're looking for him." He stood up and grabbed his helmet. "Well, I gotta go collect rent from my paying tenants."

"Why didn't you tell him abou ̶ Taryn asked when he was gone.

"For what?" Yaya shrugged.

"I still say you're making a mistak ̶ Especially when you know Paige is ̶ here," Monya added. "You're asking ̶

"Look, if Paige is legit, then Celes ̶ a threat to her, right?" Yaya put he ̶ her hip. She didn't know why they we ̶ "I don't see a problem, unless th ̶ truth to what Celeste said about Pa ̶ gold-digging skank. I can't believe ̶ her daughter off on *Q* like he's he ̶ something. Celeste says it's ridiculou ̶ tell, and she's just helping me look o ̶ cy's best interest. Besides, I know ̶ better than anyone, and there's no w ̶ with Paige is serious. If it was, he wo ̶ to me about her before now. She's ̶ one of his 'in-betweens,' you'll see.' ̶

"All I see is a whole lot of dra ̶ unfold, and when it does, you are ̶ one your brother is looking at," Ta ̶

Chapter 13

"Wow, you look stunning!" Quincy said when she came downstairs.

"And you look dashing!" she said, admiring the custom-fit tuxedo he was wearing.

Paige knew this was a night he had been looking forward to for weeks. When he told her he was being honored by the Chamber of Commerce as their Businessman of the Year, she screamed, "I am so proud of you!"

"We'd better get going or we're gonna be late."

"It's only six-fifteen. The dinner doesn't start until seven-thirty." Paige checked her watch.

"You know the Businessman of the Year can't come strolling in at seven-thirty, girl. I have to be there early to get a good seat."

"You have a whole reserved table, fool." Paige laughed.

It was still early when they arrived at the banquet. Quincy held her hand and introduced her to several of his associates who were standing in the lobby.

She felt so proud to be with him. He was so personable, and everyone had something good to say about him. Paige also loved the fact that when he looked at her, she could see the way he felt about her in his eyes.

He put his hand in the small of her back as they made their way to their table, causing tingles to run up and down her spine. "Look, there's Yaya." Quincy pointed to his sister who had walked in.

Paige observed the elegance of her stride, her form-fitting champagne gown clinging to her small body. As she walked across the room, all eyes were on her. There was no doubt in Paige's mind—Yaya was a bona fide diva in her own right. Her hair was pulled in a perfect upsweep, a few scattered curls in just the right places. Her make-up was flawless. The perfection of Yaya's presence was so apparent; even Paige looked down at her own ivory gown to see if it was sufficient.

"Your sister looks a lot like Lela Rochon," Paige whispered.

"I've heard that more than a few times." Quincy laughed, his eyes remaining on Yaya. "Lela Rochon and Janet Jackson—I've heard both of those, but they don't look anything alike."

"They're both beautiful, and so is your sister."

"You always cause a scene, huh, Yaya?" Quincy stood to greet his sister.

"How did I cause a scene?" Yaya asked innocently.

"I'm supposed to be the man of the hour, but all eyes are on you." He held her chair out.

"She can't help being the belle of the ball; it comes naturally?—Isn't that right, Yaya?" Paige laughed.

"That's right—If you can't handle the competition, then get out of the game," Yaya said politely.

If Paige didn't know any better, she would have thought the comment was aimed at her. "He's right, though—you do look beautiful," she told her.

"Thank you, Paige," Yaya replied, her voice stiff. "You look nice as well. Your face is gorgeous. Who did it?"

"Taryn hooked me up this afternoon."

Something flickered in Yaya's eyes. "Taryn?"

"Yeah. She came by the house and did it. I made the appointment with her the other day. I was glad she answered the phone because I had been leaving messages for her with the receptionist, but she never called me back. I see business is going well. That's good."

"Yes, it is." Yaya nodded. "Hopefully, the Chamber of Commerce will be presenting me with one of these awards one of these days."

"Following in your big brother's footsteps, huh?" Quincy winked. "You always were a copy-cat."

"For now, but soon you're gonna be eating my dust." Yaya stuck her tongue out at him.

Watching the two of them go back and forth made Paige wish she hadn't been an only child.

The three of them made small talk until the program began.

The dinner was bland, but hearing Quincy's name being called as the honoree of the night made up for it. It took all the self-control Yaya had to keep her composure and not scream, "Go, baby," as he walked and stood behind the podium to receive his award.

"When I opened my first barbershop five years ago, I did it with a purpose in mind. For me, *Q*-Masters was a way to provide a service *to* the community while providing employment within the community. I grew up in a family that instilled values, friendship, and a strong work ethic while giving loving care in a safe environment. These days, a lot of our young men don't have the opportunity to gain what I did from their own families, but they can gain it from the community, which includes *Q*-Masters. That's the same goal and same approach I have with each shop that I open: to instill values, friendship, and work ethic in a caring, safe environment. For me, *Q*-Masters was never about money; it was giving back. And that's what I encourage each of you business owners to do—give back.

"None of this would be possible without God, who trusted me with this responsibility. I want to thank the Chamber for this award, it lets me know that none of my hard work has been in vain. I also want to thank my sister, Yaya, who has embarked on her own journey to make her mark in the world—I love you, Yaya.

"I also want to thank my girlfriend, Paige, who has been a constant encouragement for me without even knowing she is. You are one of a kind, and I love you. Thank you, everyone."

Applause thundered as people rose to their feet, giving Quincy a standing ovation.

Paige dabbed at the tears that had formed in her eyes. Quincy Westbrooke was a wonderful man, and she was blessed to have him in her life. She beamed with pride as she watched Quincy pose for pictures with other leaders of the community.

Oddly, Yaya remained seated. There was something strange about the way she was looking at her brother. It was as if she was in shock.

"Are you okay?" Paige leaned over and asked her.

"I'm fine," Yaya said, stoically. Her demeanor had changed; she was no longer friendly. "I have to leave. Tell my brother I will talk to him later."

"Yaya, wait." Paige was confused.

Yaya rose and walked out of the ballroom without saying another word.

Paige turned her attention back to Quincy, who was still smiling as the cameras flashed. Something had to have happened within the last five minutes that caused Yaya to become upset. What it was, Paige didn't know.

"Did she say anything before she left?" Quincy asked, when she told him what happened.

"No. She just said she had to leave and she would call you later. You think she's okay?"

"Yeah. She probably went to meet Jason." Quincy shrugged. "I'll call her when I get home."

"I'm so proud of you, *Q*."

He reached over and took Paige's hand. "I meant every word I said. You don't know how much you mean to me."

"I'm sure you can show me later." Paige winked.

"You'd better believe it. You know a brother is always down for climbing some stairs."

"I can meet you tomorrow," Tia called Paige's cell and told her the following morning. Quincy was taking a shower, and she was still lying in bed, recuperating from their fulfilling night.

"You're kidding," Paige said. She knew Tia said it wouldn't take that long, but she wasn't expecting her call for a few days.

After talking to Tia more in-depth, and looking at it from a business aspect, Paige realized that refinancing the house was a smart move. She even began thinking of what she could do with the money.

"Nope. You want to come here in the morning?"

"How about we meet for lunch?" Paige suggested.

"That's fine with me. You want me to call him, or do you want to do the honors?"

"Let me do it. You haven't mentioned it to him, have you?"

"Nope. He doesn't have a clue."

"Great." Paige snickered.

She knew Marlon was going to be livid when he found out, and she was glad. She agreed on a time and place to meet and wasted no time calling Marlon.

"Hey there. What's up, sweetie?" he answered.

"I was thinking maybe we could do lunch tomorrow," she told him, when she heard the shower running.

"Tomorrow? What time?"

"How about one o'clock?" She hoped he didn't already have plans. Even if he did, she was going to make sure he changed them.

"One is good. Where?"

Relieved, she answered, "Fat Tuesdays?"

"Our spot." He laughed. "You're not trying to re-live old times, are you?"

"You never know."

"I'll see you tomorrow afternoon, and we can definitely talk about them," he told her. "I can't wait."

I bet you can't, you jerk. "Neither can I!"

Chapter 14

"What happened to you last night? Why did you dip like that?"

Yaya had overslept and was rushing to get to work. Her schedule was packed for the day, and she didn't have time to talk to Quincy right then. "I was tired. I told your girlfriend to tell you I would call."

"I know. She told me. But you could've waited a few more minutes and said something to me? If I woulda dipped out on you like that, you would still be yelling in my ear."

"I really didn't think you'd notice, Q. It's not like I didn't show up at all. I was there for the important part, and I heard your little speech as you gushed about your new girlfriend, giving her her props and all." Yaya looked around for her shoes.

"What are you talking about, Yaya? You know I didn't gush about anybody, and I gave you your props as well. Why are you hating?"

"I'm not hating, *Q*—that's not my style. And speaking of style—what's up with you and that girl?"

"What girl?"

"Paige—Don't act like you don't know who I'm talking about," she huffed as she searched for her keys.

"What do you mean, what's up with her?— She's my girlfriend. Do you have a problem with her? . . . Because that's what it's sounding like."

"*Q*, you announced that you love her in front of two hundred people." Yaya double-checked her reflection in the mirror as she walked out the door.

"I do love her," he said matter-of-factly.

It was the first time in a long time that she had heard her brother say that about a woman, and although she was glad to hear he had finally fallen in love, she didn't like the fact that it was with a woman who was out to use him.

"You don't love her, Quincy. You don't even know her like that."

"I know her better than you think, Yaya. Paige is a remarkable woman, who I enjoy a lot."

"You've enjoyed a lot of women, Quincy." Yaya hit the lock on her car and opened the door.

"Are you just now leaving the house? It's after nine o'clock," he said, sounding surprised.

"I know what time it is, *Q*—Don't start. And the only reason I'm asking about Paige is because she's not your usual type. You know how you usually date those tall, Amazonian, anorexic-looking chicks."

"That's not funny."

"Tell me I'm lying then." Yaya laughed.

"I will admit, most of the women I've dated in the past have been tall and athletic."

"And dark."

"Not true."

"Yes, it is. They all fit the same mold. Barbie-doll chicks."

"And I never came close to feeling about them the way I feel about Paige."

"Quincy, she's not on your level. I think she has ulterior motives. She sees a successful brother like you and knows that you'll be a good provider for her and her child. You've said it to me time and time again. The reason you don't date single moms is because of all the drama that comes with them."

"You're right, Yaya, but I love Paige enough to deal with any drama she may have."

"So, you admit that she has some issues?"

"All women have issues, including you." He laughed.

"You know what I mean, Quincy; I'm telling you, she's not the one," Yaya said into the phone.

"And I'm telling you, she is. I don't know what your beef is with Paige, but you need to check it. She's done nothing to even make you act like this."

Thinking about all the things Celeste had told her about Paige over the past few days made Yaya think otherwise. She knew that Quincy was not trying to hear anything she had to say about his beloved Paige. She was going to have to find a way for him to see for himself.

"I'm done talking about this, Q. I'm just telling you not to go and do anything stupid, like buying a ring because you think you know, but you have no idea."

"Wow, Yaya, is that an original line? I coulda swore I heard it on MTV," he snickered.

She hung up without saying good-bye.

As she walked into the salon, she instantly knew something was going on. Monya was wearing a strange look, and Taryn and Celeste weren't anywhere around. Two customers were waiting.

Yaya greeted them and then asked, "What's up? Where's T?"

"Uh, she and Celeste—"

Suddenly, she heard Taryn's voice coming from the back. "I'm warning you, you don't wanna cross me!"

"What in the world?" Yaya walked to Taryn's office, which was right beside hers. The door was open, and she looked inside to see Celeste standing in front of an obviously upset Taryn, who was standing on the other side of the desk. "What's up?"

Taryn looked up at her, her eyes full of anger. "For some reason, a certain person has been unable to make an appointment with me."

"She's lying," Celeste said softly. "She hasn't called to make an appointment."

Yaya knew they had to be talking about Paige. "What is she talking about, Celeste?"

"Paige told her that she's been calling for a week, trying to make an appointment and left messages for Taryn." Celeste turned and looked at Yaya. "I wouldn't dare turn business away!"

She looked so pitiful, Yaya felt sorry for her. She didn't know who to believe, Paige or Celeste. She decided to protect her employee. "*T*, that may be true. Celeste has only been working part-time. I've been manning the phones, and I haven't received a call from Paige either."

Taryn stared at both of them. "I have customers waiting. Celeste, you don't know me, but Yaya does, and she will tell you that if you fuck with my money, I will fuck with you. I'm running a business here, and I don't have time for petty games. Whatever issues you have with anyone that walks through that door, you better leave them in the damn parking lot before you come in—that goes for both of you. Understood?"

"Yes," Celeste said, her voice barely above a whisper as she turned and sulked out the door.

Yaya stared at Taryn, her best friend, shocked that she would dare speak to her that way—and in front of Celeste. *This chick is on some ego trip. I don't know what the hell Lincoln has been feeding into her head, but it's caused her to lose her damn mind.*

"*T*, I think you're overreacting."

"I don't care what you think, Yaya. You didn't care about what I thought when you hired her."

The day dragged on. For the first time the usual laughter and relaxed atmosphere was no longer present in the salon. A few of the customers even noticed.

Tam, one of Monya's regular customers asked, "Who died?"

"Huh?" Monya looked up from the acrylic she was using.

"I mean, it's so quiet and drab in here. I thought maybe someone had died." Tam shrugged.

"No one died, Tam." Monya looked over at Taryn, who was doing a manicure.

"Then you all need to stop acting like it. Hell, I coulda went to the Asian nail shop over on Patterson and been bored. I come in here to be entertained." Tam laughed. "And to hear the latest word on the street. Now, Ms. Taryn, what's up with you and what's his name—Lincoln?"

"Yeah, Taryn, what's up with you and Lincoln?" Monya repeated, relieved someone tried to ease the tension.

"Why you gotta be asking about me?" Taryn giggled.

"Because inquiring minds wanna know. Spill it," Tam demanded.

"Well, I've decided to play it cool, you know," Taryn said. "Let him know I'm interested in a subtle way."

Yaya decided to join in. "Is panting every time he walks through the door subtle?"

She too was annoyed by the silence. She had just finished arching a set of eyebrows and had another customer waiting. Celeste had left early, saying she had a headache.

Taryn's jaw dropped in an obvious false look of astonishment. "I do not pant, Yaya. You are just jealous, that's all."

"Jealous of what?"

"That he doesn't give you the same attention he gives me when he comes in."

Everyone laughed, and things seemed to be coming back to normal.

"I should get my brows done," Tam commented, admiring Yaya's work. "How much is that, Taryn?"

"For you, Tam, a hundred dollars—you need a little extra work." Taryn laughed.

Tam laughed too. "Let me ask the professional—Yaya, how much to get my brows done?"

"Depends on how you want 'em."

"What do you mean?"

"If you want them plucked or done with a razor, it's ten. If you want them threaded, then it's fifteen."

Yaya explained the difference in the techniques and then added, "I also can do your lashes, girl. I can add some extensions to them so good, they look better than a weave."

"For real? Let me splurge on myself for a change, something I rarely do."

"Why not?" Monya told her.

"Girl, you know when you have a child, you no longer have the ability to indulge," Tam told her. "The only person who gets splurges is my son."

"Okay, okay," Yaya told her. "Now you're making me feel bad. If you want them done, I'll hook you up with a discount."

"Now that's what's up," Tam squealed.

"I bet your man still splurges on himself, even though y'all have a child—You know how men are," Taryn said.

"Well, my man and my baby daddy are two different people." Tam giggled.

"That explains a lot right there," Yaya said. "I can't stand deadbeat dads."

"My son's father isn't a deadbeat at all; he's a great provider for my son. He goes above and beyond his call of duty. I definitely can't complain about him. Hell, I can depend on him more than I can my boyfriend."

"Then why isn't your son's father your boyfriend?" Monya asked.

"Because we get along better as friends than lovers. Sounds crazy, huh?" Tam laughed.

"Yeah, it does." Yaya said, finishing the client she as working on.

Tam took a seat in her chair.

Yaya carefully shaped her eyebrows until they were perfect. "You have nice eyes," she told her, passing her the mirror when she finished.

"I love it. My boyfriend ain't gonna know how to act, when I get to his house. I'm 'bout to be batting my eyes while I'm getting my groove on."

"You'd better chill before you wind up with *two* baby daddies," Yaya warned her.

"Nope. Now if things keep going the way they are, I'll have a baby daddy *and* a husband." Tam reached into her purse and handed Yaya her money.

"You're getting married?"

"I'm damn sure trying to. When I met my boyfriend, I knew he was just what I had been praying for. Being his wife is my number one goal." Tam waved as she walked out the door. "See you next week, girlfriends. And can the party already be jumping before I arrive?"

"That girl is a fool," Taryn said.

"True, dat," Monya agreed. "It's customers like her that make my day go fast!"

"She's one-of-a-kind, that's for sure," Yaya said.

Chapter 15

Celeste answered the phone. "After Effex, where the after is better than the before." Yaya cringed as she messed the slogan up for the ninetieth time. "Yeah, she right here. Monya, phone." Celeste lay the phone on the reception area. "Uh, can you see I'm busy?" Monya looked up from the set of hands she was working on. "My bad." Celeste picked the phone back up. "She's busy. Can I take a message?"

Yaya rummaged through her black leather make-up cases. "FedEx still hasn't gotten here?" Running low on several supplies, she had placed an order almost a week earlier, and it still hadn't arrived. She had two big events to do this weekend, and she needed to be prepared.

Celeste hung the phone up and flipped through a magazine. "No, not yet."

"Did you go call them yesterday like I asked you, Celeste?"

"You didn't tell me to call FedEx." She continued reading, not even bothering to look up.

"Celeste, I did tell you to call them." Yaya frowned. "I wrote the order number and tracking numbers down and handed them to you before I left."

"Oh, I thought you wanted me to call M·A·C—that's who I called; they said your order was shipped out three days ago."

"I know that my order was shipped three days ago—How the hell do you think I got the tracking number?" Yaya snapped, causing everyone in the shop to look at her. "You know what—just forget it. I'll do it my damn self."

She closed the case and walked back into her office, plopping onto the chair behind her desk. She began looking through the mass of papers for the number for FedEx. Her stomach was aching; she hadn't felt well at all the past few days. She told herself it was just stress. Between the successes of the shop, photo shoots she had already committed herself to, and the upcoming events, she was probably wearing herself too thin. She opened her drawer and found a bottle of Aleve and popped three pills.

"Headache?"

She thought she was imagining things when she heard Jason's voice. She glanced up to see that indeed he was standing in the doorway of her office.

It was the first time she had seen him in a while. They talked a few times since then, but not as frequently as she would like. And every so often, he would come to her house for a much-needed bedroom rendezvous. She was determined not to sweat him, though. He said he needed space, and she was going to give it to him. When he did call, she was as cheerful as ever. And when she called him, she made sure not to seem as if she was concerned about where he was or what he was doing with whom, even though she thought about it constantly. She told herself to just give it some time, and they would be back together soon enough.

Now, as he stood in front of her looking like he had just stepped off the cover of *GQ* magazine, she thought, *God, he is fine.*

She stood up and smoothed the front of her shirt down. "Not anymore." She smiled and walked over to him.

He took her into his arms and pulled her to him. Her arms reached around his neck, and she held him tight as they embraced.

"You're looking good." He kissed her cheek.

"Now, you're lying," she told him, "but I'll take the compliment."

"I can see you're working hard. It's a nice amount of people out there." He nodded.

"Yeah. We stay busy, that's for sure. Taryn and I are actually about to hire two more nail techs."

"Already? Wow! I'm impressed."

"Yeah. We stay booked, and you know this is the busiest season for our make-up bookings. We really didn't expect to have to hire anyone until after Labor Day, but if we don't, we're gonna have to turn people away."

"And you definitely don't want that to happen."

"Exactly. So what brings you to this side of town?"

"What makes you think I didn't want to come and see you?"

"Because I know better."

"No, seriously. I came to see you." Jason shrugged and touched her hair softly.

"I'm glad you did."

"So you have any plans for next Saturday?" he asked.

Her first instinct was to tell him no, but she decided to play it cool. "Let me check my calendar." She walked behind her desk and flipped through her day planner to the following Friday's date, which she already knew was empty. "No, I don't see where I have anything scheduled."

"Good." He smiled. "Would you consider having dinner with me?"

"I'd love to have dinner with you, Jason." She was so elated that she had to stop herself from grinning from ear to ear. *Play it cool, Yaya. Don't be pressed.*

"I'll pick you up at eight then." He smiled, looked down at his watch. "I have a meeting in about an hour, but I will call you later."

"I'll talk to you then. Let me walk you out."

He took her by the hand, and she walked him back through the shop. All eyes were on them as they exited out the front door. She knew that she and Jason would be the topic of conversation when she returned.

"So I guess I'll see you Friday then?"

He opened the door to his silver Range Rover. "You may see me before then." He smiled. He leaned over and kissed her gently, and got in.

She closed his door and walked back inside, making sure to put a sway into her hips, in case he was still looking.

"I see someone is in a better mood," Taryn said, as soon as she stepped through the door.

"Shut up." Yaya grinned. "You'd be in a bad mood too if you had a hair book shoot and a wedding to do this weekend and your brushes look like mine. Not to mention, I barely have any cremestick liners. Are you gonna loan me yours?"

"You know better than that," Taryn said with the quickness. "I got three faces to do myself on Saturday for a bachelor party."

"Then you should be a little more sympathetic to my situation." Yaya noticed that there were empty sections of nail colors on the shelves. "Are we out of colors already?"

"No, we have stock in the back that hasn't been opened, I think." Monya eyed Celeste, who was sitting in the same spot and looking at the same magazine that she was before Yaya went into her office.

One thing Yaya had learned quickly was that as beneficial as Celeste was in the gossip department, she was as lazy in the work department. Yaya constantly had to tell her what to do, and if she wasn't told to do it, it wasn't getting done.

"Celeste, you've gotta keep these shelves stocked. There shouldn't be any empty spots up here," Yaya told her.

"I tried to explain that day before yesterday," Taryn added.

"Oh, my bad. I'll go get it and restock the shelves." She slowly rose out of her seat and trotted to the back, returning with two boxes of nail polish.

"Go ahead and replace the bottles with just a little color in them as well," Yaya advised her.

"What do you want me to do with the old bottles?"

"Just put them in a bag and put them on my desk. I'll figure something out later." Yaya watched as Celeste put the bottles on the shelves.

"Why do you have to do faces for a bachelor party, Taryn?" one of the customers asked. "The groom needs make-up or something?"

"No." Taryn laughed, along with Monya and Yaya. "The entertainment does."

"You're kidding," the woman said. "The strippers?"

"You better believe it," Taryn told her. "They are some of Yaya's and my best customers . . . isn't that right?"

"She's right," Yaya told her. "They really are. And I must admit, some of my most beautiful ones."

"I can't believe you do make-up for strippers." The lady frowned. "What? Do they swing by here on their way to the club?"

Yaya could see the hurt in Monya's eyes and answered, "Our clients are professionals who require professional treatment, and they are paying customers just like everyone else that walks through these doors. I wouldn't be so quick to judge."

Little did the woman know, Monya, herself, used to be a dancer at one point. It wasn't something she was proud of, but it wasn't something she was ashamed of either. That was actually how the three of them met—Monya was a dancer in a rap video that both Yaya and Taryn worked on.

"I'm just saying, I thought you all were high-class make-up artists, that's all."

"We are," Taryn told her. "As a matter of fact, we are the most sought-after image consultants in the business."

"Then why did you open a salon down here rather than in some glitzy upscale place?"

"Because if we would've done that, we wouldn't be able to service our class of clientele, such as yourself," Monya said, as she finished the woman's nails.

"And what class is that?" The woman paid Monya.

"The cheap class." Monya smiled and held the door open for the woman to exit.

"I guess she won't be coming back." Taryn laughed.

"Probably not. But I have twelve other people waiting to get into that chair, and they tip a hell of a lot better than she does," Monya replied. "I'm starving."

"Me too," Yaya agreed. "Monya, you should go to Ochie's and get us some food."

"I'm not going all the way down to Ochie's. Besides, I have two more appointments. You should go."

Yaya looked at her like she was crazy. "You know I'm not going down there! *T*, what time is your next appointment?"

"Yaya, just get into your car and go get the food. It's only like fifteen minutes away," Taryn told her.

"You're crazy, and I drove the Lex today too! Now, I could see if I drove the Honda."

"No, you're the crazy one."

Taryn and Monya laughed.

"What's so funny?"

They all looked up to see Fitzgerald coming through the door with a dolly, carrying a stack of boxes. He was dressed in the same brown uniform he had been wearing the first day she met him.

"What's up, Fitz?" Taryn greeted him.

"About damn time!" Yaya snapped. "These boxes should've been here two days ago. What? Have you been riding around with them in your truck for a few days because you recognized the address?"

"Hold the hell on. You need to check your-self—These boxes just got there this morning. I knew I was coming over here to get a line-up, so I grabbed them to deliver. I called myself doing you a favor because they weren't scheduled to be put on a damn truck until late this evening, which meant you wouldn't have gotten them until tomorrow sometime!"

Fitzgerald stood in front of her.

They stared at each other. Yaya was deter-mined not to be intimidated by the intensity in his eyes.

"Thanks, Fitz." Taryn's voice interrupted their staring contest.

"It's not a problem." His eyes finally broke away from hers. He leaned to slide the boxes off the dolly.

"Can you go ahead and take them to the storage room in the back for me?" Yaya asked.

Fitz didn't answer her. He held out the brown electric clipboard. "Sign here."

Yaya bit her tongue as she signed her name. She looked at the boxes and grabbed the top one and stormed to the storage area.

A few moments later, Fitzgerald was right be-hind her with the remaining boxes on the dolly.

"You could've brought all of those back here for me while you were trying to be funny."

"I ain't do this for you, believe that. Taryn asked me to bring these back here, so I obliged. Where do they need to go?"

"You can leave them there because I have to go through them and get what I need out. Do you have a blade?"

"What?" He seemed offended by her question.

"A knife, a blade . . . something I can use to open these with." Yaya sighed.

"Oh, yeah, right here." He reached into his belt and removed a large cutter.

"Thanks." She took it from him.

"Wow! I can't believe you actually know how to use those words."

"What are you saying?" The sharp blade made a slick noise as she used it to open the first box, removing the invoice lying right inside and rummaging through white pieces of foam, to make sure all her items were there.

"I'm saying that you are so demanding and sharp-tongued all the time that I didn't know you could actually be appreciative about something."

"Are you saying I'm bitchy?" She reached for another box.

"You said it, I didn't." He slid the box over to her so she could open it.

"I don't think I'm bitchy."

Once again, she opened the box and checked it.

"What do you call it then?" He grabbed the blade from the shelf and began opening another box and passing her the inventory sheet.

"I call it being *stern*." She looked closely at the paper.

"I think it's a little more than stern."

They continued talking until all the boxes had been opened. "Where is the last box?"

"This is it," Fitz told her.

"There has to be another box. I have missing items. And the last box says it's five of six," she said, becoming irritated.

The missing box contained the items she knew she would need most this weekend. Frustration crept into her body.

"I'm telling you, there were only five boxes for you. I double-checked myself."

"I have missing stuff. I need my product to work with. What the hell am I gonna do?"

"When I get back to the—"

"You know what—you've helped enough for the day, Fitz. Don't even worry about it."

Once again, there was a pain in her stomach, and she felt hot. Yaya brushed past Fitz and walked into her office, closing the door. She sat down and laid her head on her desk.

There was a small knock at the door.

"Yeah."

The door opened, and Taryn stepped in. "Yaya, what's wrong?"

"I just don't feel good, that's all." Yaya didn't lift her head. She could feel her friend's "cool hands" on her neck.

"You don't feel warm. What hurts?"

"My stomach and my head," Yaya mumbled.

"It's probably because you're hungry." Taryn sighed.

"No, that's not it. They didn't ship all my product. I have that shoot for Larry Scott on Friday, and I have a whole wedding party to do on Saturday."

"Yaya, you know, whatever you need, if I got it, you got it. Don't even stress about it. Look, we've got everything under control here at the salon. Why don't you go home and relax for a while?"

Yaya looked up at her best friend and saw the worry in her face. "I'm good, T. Really."

"Are you sure?"

"Yeah, I am." Yaya smiled at her.

"You know you were wrong for dogging Fitz out like that, don't you?"

"I ain't dog him out."

"From the way he stormed out of here, you did something to him."

"What did he say?"

"Something about your being a ungrateful, stern, and I ain't even gonna say the other word he used." Taryn laughed. "But put it this way—it begins with a *b*, and rhymes with *rich*."

Yaya smiled. She knew that she was rude to Fitz, but didn't think she was that bad. "Hell, he should meet some of the models and artists I have to work with, and then maybe he'll see I'm damn near a nun compared to them."

"Why do you act like that around him?" Taryn asked.

Yaya really didn't have an answer. It was something about Fitzgerald that made her uncomfortable. When he looked at her, it was as if he was trying to see everything inside her head or read her mind. And when she stared into his eyes, she felt as if she was being hypnotized.

"I don't act any different around him than I do anyone else. You sound crazy." Yaya stood. "Come on, let's go talk Monya into going to Ochie's for us."

Chapter 16

Paige walked up to the bar and greeted Marlon. "Have you been waiting long?"

He turned and smiled at her. "Not long at all. You look nice," he said, rising off the stool.

She gave him a hug, and he tenderly kissed her on the forehead, something he had always done. She caught a whiff of his Hugo Boss cologne. For a fleeting moment, she closed her eyes, and it was like old times between them, but she stopped herself before she even got caught up in thinking about the past. *Don't forget why we're here, girl. Remain focused—he's still the same old triflin' Marlon.*

"Thank you. You want to go ahead and get a table?"

"Yeah, we can." Marlon grinned.

The hostess seated them at a table in the back of the restaurant, and they sat down. "You want a drink?"

"No, I'm good."

"So tell me, to what do I owe the honor of this meeting?— What's up?" Marlon sat back.

"Well, it's sort of a celebration lunch."

"What are we celebrating?" He looked at her curiously. "Don't tell me you're about to get married or something. I know you didn't bring me here to tell me some nonsense like that."

"No, that's not it at all. And, if I was, at least that would show more respect than you have for me; I had to hear about your marriage from Camille. And let's not talk about the fact that you were still trying to get back with me, when you up and got married."

"I don't even wanna talk about that right now. Don't try to change the subject." He sighed.

"You were the one that brought the subject of marriage up. I'm curious though. Why is it a mess?"

"Don't go there, Paige. Come on now, tell me what's going on. What's this supposed celebration for?"

"Hold on. I'm about to tell you right now." Paige spotted Tia walking through the door of the restaurant. "We are celebrating the refinance of our house!"

Marlon looked as if he was about to throw up, when Tia walked up and said, "Hi there!"

"Hey, girl, have a seat," Paige told her. "I really appreciate you meeting us down here."

"It wasn't a problem at all." Tia smiled. "Hey, Marlon."

"What the hell is this about?"

"Well, Tia was nice enough to meet us so we can sign the paperwork and get our checks at the same time. That way, it would be no delay on anyone's part. Right, Tia?"

"That's right." Tia placed a brown leather briefcase on the table and popped it open. She removed some stacks of paperwork and closed it back up. "I was able to get you guys a great rate, like I promised both of you."

"I knew you would, girl. Marlon, I can't believe how much equity we had in that house."

He glared at her. "Paige, what the hell are you talking about?"

"Well, when the mortgage broker from the bank called to verify my information, I thought, why use him when my cousin works for the same company? So, I called Tia, and she took care of everything for us. Good thing the other guy called because you forgot to tell me about re-financing the house. I guess with your "mess" of a marriage and everything else going on, it slipped your mind. Nevertheless, she was able to get it done, and here we are at the celebration lunch."

"I just need for you to sign here and here, Paige." Tia pointed to the papers and gave her a pen. Paige signed her name with flair and then passed the papers to Marlon.

"I can't believe you're doing this to me, Paige," he said to her, his eyes full of anger.

"I can't believe a lot of things you've done to me, Marlon. That house was supposed to be an investment for both of us, and you try to go behind my back and steal from me? That's like taking money from Myla. The only time we were going to borrow on that house was to pay for her education. And then you tried to do it behind my back?"

"Paige, things are just hard for me right now. Kasey's not working because she is there taking care of my mother."

"Your mother's not sick, Marlon; she was fine the last time I saw her—she was drunk, but that's always been the case. I don't want to hear any of this. Hell, it's been a rough time for me too. I had to start over myself, but I would never ever go behind your back and do what you tried to do to me."

Marlon looked over at Tia for support, but found none.

"Look, I've known both of you for a long time," Tia said. "Marlon, you know going behind Paige's back was dead wrong. She could actually have you arrested for fraud. You signed her name on a loan application. I don't know what to say about that. If times were that hard, you should've gone to her and explained that you needed some cash and the only way you could see you could get it was to re-finance the house."

"She would've said no," he said.

"You don't know that. Maybe she would've; maybe not. But at least you would have given her the respect of talking to her, before you made a big decision like that behind her back. So, now you have your money. It may only be half of what you thought you were gonna get, but that's better than none. So, sign right here so I can give you both your checks and leave."

As Marlon scribbled his name, Tia reached inside the manilla folder, passing each of them a large, business-size check.

Paige folded hers and put it in her purse without even looking at it; Marlon just slipped his into his pocket.

"Thanks, Tia." Paige leaned over and hugged her.

"No problem. I'll be praying for both of you, and I'm still here for both of you. Call me if you need anything," she said, rising from the table.

"I don't believe this," Marlon said, after she was gone.

"Don't start, Marlon." Paige grabbed her purse and prepared to leave as well. "It's over and done. You have over a hundred thousand dollars in your pocket, and the mortgage is even cheaper—you'll get by."

"I don't want to get by—I want to get *out*."

Paige shook her head and looked at him. "Then get out, Marlon. I don't know why you got in it in the first place. Nobody made you to marry that woman."

"You don't get it." He shook his head.

"Oh, I get it—I got it for seven years—You were the one who didn't get it. And if you still don't see what the problem is, then you deserve to stay there."

Paige reached into her purse and pulled out her shades, placing them on her face to hide the tears that had formed. She didn't even know why she was crying. Marlon was no longer her problem. She had her money from the house, and that's all that mattered.

I shouldn't even be bothered by this; it's his problem. He allowed his mother to control his life, and married that tramp instead of me, and now he has to deal with it.

"Good-bye, Marlon." Page hurried out of the restaurant.

Just as she was about to get into her truck, she heard him calling her name. She paused and waited as he ran toward her.

"What?"

"I'm sorry, Paige. Believe it or not, I am really sorry. I was in a bind. I panicked and I was wrong."

"It's okay, Marlon. I hope things get better for you. I really do. But you need to do some serious soul-searching and figure out some things."

He gave her a hug, and once again, kissed her on the forehead and then the chin, as always.

Some things never change. She got in and drove off. She glanced in her rearview mirror and saw his reflection, praying he would be all right.

"It's about time you made it back into town," Paige said to Titus as he came out of the garage and met her. "We missed you."

"Who is '*we*'?" He gave her a quick hug.

"Me, Quincy, Myla."

"I hope another name is somewhere in there," he said, a touch of hope in his voice.

"Nina." She winked at him.

"Quit lying." He laughed. "So how've things been going?"

"They are going good, real good. Good enough for me to buy something really nice."

"I heard you were interested in buying something really nice. *Q* ain't tell me you were coming by here and getting it today though."

"He doesn't know I was coming by here. I do want to get the car though, Titus—today. Can I write you a check?"

"For you, it's a done deal. Let me go get your keys. You can trail me to the DMV, and we can take care of the paperwork. Man, you wouldn't believe how many calls I got about this car."

"I knew from the moment I laid eyes on it, it was mine." She wrote him a check, knowing that after the large deposit she just made, it wouldn't dare bounce.

"So what are you gonna do with the truck?" he asked as they waited at the DMV.

"Give it to a deserving college student who can't seem to find a job." She laughed, knowing she was about to make Camille's day.

"Hey, baby. How was your day?"

"It was good. Long, but good." He kissed her. "How was yours?"

"It was awesome!" She smiled and kissed him again.

"Wow! It must have been off the chain at the library today. What happened?—Did someone return some overdue books?"

"Oh, you got jokes, huh? Keep getting smart and I won't let you roll wit' me in my new ride."

"What new ride?"

"My new Benz, baby!" She held up her keys.

"You got the car from Titus?—Stop playing. Are you serious?" He opened the door and looked out front.

"It's not out there. I need for you to take me to pick it up from Titus' shop. He's getting it detailed and putting the tags on for me. It should be ready by the time we get there."

"I'm thinking Titus let you have the car at a decent price, right?" Quincy asked, as they got into his car and headed to Titus. "I know you said you were interested, but you weren't sure about getting the money yet."

"He gave me a better than fair price, *Q*. He would have had to hear your mouth if he didn't."

"So are you gonna be able to handle two car payments?"

"I went ahead and paid my truck off today, so I won't have two payments. As a matter of fact, I won't have a payment at all."

"That's what's up—you got Titus to sell your truck for you?"

"No. I'm giving the truck to Camille; she needs a car to get around in."

"But you paid for the Benz, straight-up. And you paid off your truck."

"Yep, I'm financially savvy like that." Paige was tempted to tell him about the check she'd received from re-financing, but recalled their last conversation in regards to the whole Marlon and the house situation. She decided that not volunteering any additional info was her best bet.

"Okay, Ms. Financially Savvy. I'm glad you were able to get your car. You deserve it." He reached over and took her by the hand. "I'm proud of you."

"Thanks, baby. That means a lot coming from you."

"Paige, you know how much I care about you, right?" Quincy asked as they pulled into the parking lot of the garage.

She was bewildered by the question. For some reason, it seemed to come from nowhere. "I care about you too, Quincy. I love you, you know that."

"I love you too. I just don't want you to think that I ever take our relationship for granted. I know without a doubt how special you are and how lucky I am to have you in my life." He stared at her.

The emotion in his voice brought tears to her eyes.

"I just need to know that you feel the same way. If you're having any doubts or fears about us, or the way things are going, I want you to be honest and tell me."

"*Q*, where is this coming from? I feel exactly the way that you do, if not more so. I thank God every day for bringing us together."

"I just wanted to tell you, that's all." He smiled.

Paige shook her head and took his face into her hands. She pulled his head to her, closed her eyes and kissed him, slowly. His lips seemed to be made just for hers, and she enjoyed it immensely. As her hands fell to his shoulders, she rubbed her nose against his and opened her eyes. "I love you."

"I love you too."

"You're still not driving my new Benz though," she teased, as she got out of the car.

Chapter 17

"Come on, Monya, you promised," Yaya whined. Monya promised to pick her up and take her to Ochie's, but now she was reneging, complaining about having cramps and being tired.

"Yaya, just get in your car and go. I'm tired, my stomach hurts, and I'm going to bed."

"Fine, Monya." She hung up the phone. She walked into her room and lay across her bed. She was starving, and she was still pissed about her missing FedEx package. She even left the salon and went to FedEx herself, but they didn't have an answer, and promised that they would call as soon as they located the box.

Ochie's was just what she needed. There was no way she was driving to the Bottoms by herself. She looked over at the clock and knew that Taryn was not coming out of the house this late. Her stomach began rumbling. She sat up.

Taking out a pair of black sweats and a Michael Jordan jersey that she had only worn twice in three years, she got dressed. She threw on her Jordan's and grabbed a black baseball cap, pulling it tight on her head. She grabbed the keys to her Honda and walked into her garage. She hardly ever drove this car and noticed the immaculate condition it was still in as she removed the cover she kept on it.

She opened the door and climbed in. She smiled as she recalled all the good times she and Taryn had riding around in what was known as the "*creep*mobile," after she got the Lexus. Whenever they wanted to be incognito, it was the vehicle of choice. *Those were the good old days.*

She started the engine and eased out the driveway. She cut the radio on and her Mary J. Blige's *My Life* CD began blasting. Rolling with the sunroof open and the music blasting, she felt free. Her relaxed feeling quickly shifted into apprehension, as she got off the interstate and entered the lower side of town. The dimly lit streets seemed even darker than she remembered, and her eyes kept darting from one side of the street to the other, praying she wouldn't run into any trouble. She was tempted to turn around, but felt a little better when she spotted the red, green, and yellow *Ochie's* sign and the well-lit parking lot.

She turned in and parked her car, making sure to lock the doors and set the alarm.

Sounds of reggae blasted as she opened the door and walked inside. People were standing throughout the club. Everyone seemed to be having a good time. The inside wasn't that big, but larger than she thought it would be. There were tables of varying sizes throughout, and there was even a full bar.

As she continued to the counter, where she noticed the "Place order here" sign, her eyes fell on a small dance floor.

"What can I get fa ya, chile?" a friendly woman asked.

Yaya couldn't help staring. The woman had the prettiest skin and whitest teeth she had ever seen. "Um, let me see . . ." Yaya looked up at the hanging menu. "A stewed chicken dinner with peas and rice and cabbage. Oh, and a side of macaroni and cheese."

"Be right out. What's your name?"

"Yaya," she answered, wondering why she wanted to know.

"Okay, Yaya. You can either wait at the bar or at a table. We'll call your name when it's ready."

"Oh, okay," Yaya said, feeling dumb for thinking the woman had ulterior motives. She walked over and stood at the bar, watching the crowd.

"Well, well, well . . . what are you doing here?—slumming?"

Yaya turned to see Fitzgerald standing next to her, drink in hand.

"I needed a drink after all the stress FedEx has put me through today."

"Yeah, right—you're the reason I'm here having a drink," he told her. "Talk about stress."

"Whatever," she said, trying not to be attracted to his smooth, chiseled, almond-colored body. It was a challenge, since the white linen shirt he wore fit so well; it seemed custom-made for him, along with the jeans hugging his behind. His dreads were pulled back, but a couple hung behind his back.

You don't like guys with dreads, she reminded herself. *Besides, he's not even tall enough for you. What is he?—Five nine? Let's not even mention the fact that he's nowhere near the chocolate color you desire in all your men. He's not even worth looking at.*

"Whatcha doing out here all alone, gal?" It was the worst fake Jamaican accent Yaya had ever heard.

She turned to see Lincoln smiling at her. "I can see you've had a few drinks, Lincoln." She checked out his sleepy eyes, corny grin, and the empty glass in his hand.

"Yeah, a brother is feeling kinda nice. Speaking of brothers—what's up with you and mine over there?"

"Uh, that would be nothing—what's up with you and Taryn?"

"Taryn . . ." He grinned. "That's my girl. She is so cute, and I can just be myself around her. She's cool."

"I'm glad to hear that."

"Well, enjoy the rest of your evening." He walked away.

"What's up, Fitz?" A small group of girls came over and spoke. Dressed in denim shorts with bright green-and-yellow fitted tops, hair braided in perfect cornrows, they looked as if they had just stepped out of a reggae video.

"Hey there, what's going on?" He smiled at them.

Yaya smacked her lips as she saw him checking them out.

"You ain't been out here in a while—you been working hard?" One girl touched his arms.

"You know I have. But I had a hell of a day today, and I needed to get out and have some fun."

"That's what's up. Let's go have fun then!" Another girl grabbed Fitz by the hand, and they all started dancing on the dance floor.

Soon, Sean Paul's "Temperature" began pumping from the speakers, and Yaya began rocking to the beat. She watched as the girls crowded around Fitz and pumped their bodies against his.

He seemed to be in his element as he danced to the beat with all three of them. Her eyes met his, and he grinned, as he wrapped his arm around the tiny waist of one of the girls.

The girl bent her body down in front of his and ground her derrière into his crotch.

He lifted his hand and beckoned for Yaya to come to him.

She didn't move.

He laughed and continued dancing.

For some reason, the longer she watched, the more irritated she became.

"Yaya!"

They continued to move to the beat in unison, the girl grinning and rubbing her arms on him.

"Yaya!"

Fitzgerald reached and pulled her to him, and the girl threw her leg around him.

"Yaya!"

She turned to see the waitress holding up a bag and pointing at her. She rushed over. "I'm sorry, I didn't even hear you calling me."

"I see." The girl laughed.

Yaya paid for her food and thanked the girl. She glanced back over her shoulder towards the dance floor, just as she exited the restaurant.

Fitzgerald and his dancers were no longer there. Making sure her keys were in hand, she walked out and got into her car. She was so preoccupied that she didn't even notice the text alert on her phone.

Once home, she took a bath, ate and got into bed, fighting thoughts of Fitzgerald as she closed her eyes and fell asleep.

"Good morning," Monya sang, when Yaya walked through the door.

"I thought you were so sick last night; you look fine this morning."

"Yaya, you know how my body gets on the first day of my period. I do feel better today. Tell you what—I'll go get you some Ochie's for lunch."

"I don't even want it anymore."

"Fine then. Taryn says she'll be in late this morning. She got a last-minute call this morning for a catalog shoot."

"Are you gonna be able to do her nail appointments?" Yaya looked at the book under Taryn's name and noticed two names listed for that morning.

"Yeah. It's gonna be tight, but as long as everyone is on time, I'm good."

"Where the hell is Celeste?"

"Haven't seen or heard from her." Monya shrugged. "It's not like she does any work while she's here anyway. You should really fire that lazy girl. She doesn't even fit the mold of what we said we wanted in a receptionist."

Yaya knew that Monya had a point. They did have a certain appeal that they had discussed wanting all of their employees to have.

Celeste did abide by the black-and-white color scheme they all wore daily, but instead of the chic, tasteful outfits that Monya, Taryn, and Yaya wore, she normally had on a pair of black jeans or knit slacks and an over-sized white shirt and a pair of black Reebok classics on her feet. Celeste never wore make-up and was basically a plain Jane, right down to the gold-colored, wire-rimmed glasses she wore.

As if she suspected she knew she was being talked about, Celeste walked through the door. "Hey, sorry I'm late."

"Good morning," Monya said, nonchalantly.

"Hey, Celeste, look, we need to talk. Come to the back with me for a minute," Yaya told her.

They went into her office. "You've gotta step up your game, Celeste. Monya and Taryn, well . . . all of us have been noticing some areas that need improving."

"I know I'm late, but I thought when you got my text and the picture, you were gonna call me back."

"What text? I didn't get a text from you."

"I sent you a text with a picture last night." Celeste nodded. "I should've known that you didn't get it, when you didn't call me back."

"Hold on, let me get my phone." Yaya walked back into the salon and grabbed her phone out of her purse. Sure enough, she saw that she had two text messages waiting for her.

"What's up, peoples?" Fitz walked in, carrying a box. He placed it in front of Yaya. "Can I get you to sign for this, please?"

Yaya couldn't help smiling. She was elated. "I thought they said this box never arrived at the terminal to be delivered."

"It arrived this morning, and I brought it straight over here because FedEx is tired of hearing you screaming about it. Now sign, so I can get outta here." He passed her the board to sign. "And you're welcome!"

"Thank you, Fitzgerald," she said, anxious to open the box. "Can I get that blade?"

He passed it to her. "I looked for you when you walked out last night, but I ain't see you. Why did you dip?"

"My food was ready," she told him as she opened the box.

"Where the hell were you last night?" Monya asked.

"Ochie's," Fitz answered.

"What? Yaya, you didn't even say anything about going to Ochie's last night. Who did you go with?"

"I went by myself."

"What? I don't believe that." Monya shook her head. "You ain't roll to the Bottoms alone, no way."

"Yeah, she was there all alone. I tried to get her to dance for me, but the young chicks kinda intimidated her, so she ain't even step on the floor. You know we were jamming to Sean Paul."

"Ha! Ha! Ha! You think Yaya was intimidated by somebody dancing? That's funny." Monya laughed.

"Hey, Yaya, you got change for a hundred?— What's up, Fitz?" Jarrod walked in and looked over at Monya. "What's so funny?"

"Fitz said that Yaya came to Ochie's last night by herself."

Jarrod started giggling. "Not Ms. Thang. I don't think so."

"That's not the funny part, though, Jarrod. He says that she was intimidated by some girls that were dancing on the floor. He thinks Yaya was too scared to dance."

Both Jarrod and Monya were laughing so hard that they were shaking.

Fitz and Yaya looked at them like they were crazy.

"Y'all are acting high." Yaya shook her head.

"We ain't blazed nothing yet," Jarrod replied. "It's too early in the morning."

"I still don't get what's funny," Fitzgerald said.

"Go ahead and show him what you got, Yaya," Jarron said to her. "Handle that."

"I don't have anything to prove, Jarrod." She reached into her purse and took out a wad of money. She counted out change for a hundred and handed it to him. "Here."

Monya got up and walked over to the surround sound and began fumbling. "You ready to handle your business, Ya? I got your back!"

"I'm telling you I don't have anything to—"

Before she could finish her sentence, the sounds of Sean Paul and Beyoncé's "Baby Boy" streamed throughout the salon.

Yaya looked from Monya, to Jarrod, and finally to Fitz, who was looking amused.

She took a deep breath and walked to the middle of the floor. Closing her eyes, she began moving her hips to the beat of the music. Soon she was gyrating and caught up in the groove. She could feel Fitzgerald's eyes on her as she swayed before him, performing the exact moves as the dancers in the video. She could feel the muscles in her calves as she stepped in the black three-inch heels she had on her feet, wishing she had on a skirt so he could see them, rather than the form-fitting slacks she wore. She strutted and stood in front of him and did the same move the young girl did the night before. Only, when she lifted her leg and placed it on his shoulder, she sexily slid down to the floor in a full split.

Fitzgerald's eyes widened; she could see the hunger in his eyes.

She swung around and gracefully stood up, blowing kisses to Monya and Jarrod.

"Whoo hoo!"

"Bravo! Encore!"

She gave Fitz a simple smile. "See, I wasn't intimidated by them. I didn't want to show them up. Thanks again for my box." She lifted the box up and headed back to her office, almost bumping into Celeste.

"I didn't know what was going on out here," she said. "I didn't know you could dance like that."

"I forgot you were back here," Yaya told her. "Take this box to my desk for me. Let me run and get my phone."

"Wow!" Fitz said, when she walked back in. He was still standing in the same spot.

"Don't you have some packages to deliver?" she asked him.

"I told you, 'The girl is bad'—Can you imagine what she's like in bed?" Jarrod nudged Fitz in the arm.

"Get out, Jarrod!" Monya yelled.

Yaya read the first text message she had received which was from Taryn saying she would be late this morning and would call later. The second one, from Celeste, sent the previous night, had two attachments. Yaya clicked on it to read them. Her eyes widened as her phone screen held a picture. It wasn't the best quality, but there was no doubt that there in front of her was Paige being kissed by a man who was not Quincy.

"I told you she was no good," Celeste said, a look of satisfaction on her face.

Chapter 18

"Okay, let me tell you about your friend," Nina said as she got into the car. Her car was giving her problems and Paige had agreed to give her a ride to work. "Who?"

"Mr. Titus," Nina replied.

"What did he do? Did he say what was wrong with your car?"

"Check this out. He calls around seven last night and tells me he's about to come over so he can look at it. I say, 'Cool.' He says he's gotta go home, take a shower and get cleaned up first, and then he'll be right there. My first thought was why was he getting cleaned up since he's coming to look at my car and will probably get dirty all over again, but I don't say anything. Let's not mention the fact that he knows I have triple *A*, and I can just have it towed."

"Did he come?"

"Why did he show up at my door, clean as a whistle? I'm talking clean, Paige. He is dressed in all white, from the baseball cap on his head to the Nike's on his feet, and he's smelling wonderful. I'm talking Joop! cologne. You know I know Joop! when I smell it."

Paige laughed. "Not decked out in all white with the Joop!, Nina."

"Girl, yes. I open the door, and I'm like, 'Where the hell are you going?' It's too early for DJ Terror's Fourth of July party, which by the way, I'm going to this year, whether you go with me or not."

"You're rambling," Paige said, "get to the point."

"So he comes inside, comments on my place, asks about Jade. I mean, Paige, he sits on the sofa like he's over there because I invited him."

"You did invite him."

"You know what I mean—like he came over to chill with me. I'm thinking, whatever it is you're thinking, little man, it's not going to work. By now, I'm telling him about the car and how crazy it's been acting. Then he asks me if I wanna go get something to eat."

"That was nice of him." Paige giggled. "He asked you out."

"He's asked me out before, and the answer is always still the same—no!"

"Nina, you should be ashamed of yourself. Here is a nice guy who is really into you. He is a successful businessman, and he's attractive."

"And all of that is true, but he's also all of five-foot, three. I'm not gonna go out with him. He needs to face it."

"So what did he finally say about your car?"

"After about an hour of making small talk, he asks to go to the restroom. I let him. He comes out and says that it's too dark for him to check it out and he'll send a tow truck to get it this afternoon. I swear, he is crazy." Nina shook her head.

"No, he's determined. I have to admire that about him."

Paige's cell began ringing. She saw it was Quincy. "Hey, baby. Good morning."

"Good morning. Are you at work yet?"

"No, I'm still on the way. You know I had to pick up Nina this morning."

"Oh yeah, I forgot about that," he said. "Listen, I'm about to send you a text message."

"Is it sexual?" She glanced over at Nina.

"No, it's not. But don't make any lunch plans because we need to talk, okay?"

"Not a problem. I'll see you then. I love you," she said.

He hung up without responding.

A few seconds later, her phone alerted her that she had a message. She opened it and nearly swerved off the road when she saw the picture of her and Marlon a few days ago at the restaurant. Although she knew that it was the simple gesture of his kissing her on the forehead, it still seemed to be an intimate moment between them. There was a second photo also of them in the parking lot—this time he was kissing her on her chin.

"Oh God!" She pulled into the nearest parking lot.

"What's wrong?" Nina asked.

Paige passed her the phone, showing the latter of the two pictures.

"Oh, damn. When was this?"

"The other day, when we got the checks." Paige shook her head in disbelief.

"Who the hell took this? Who knew you all were going?" Nina asked the exact questions Paige was thinking. "Who sent these to you?"

"Quincy."

"Damn! Did you at least tell him you were meeting Marlon for lunch?"

"No, I didn't. I swear, Nina, it's not how it looks."

"I know that. Everyone who knows you and Marlon knows that this is how he's always kissed you. On your forehead when he says hello, and on your chin when it's good-bye."

"Quincy ain't trying to hear that, Nina."

"What did he say?"

"Nothing. Just that we need to talk, that's all." Paige wanted to throw up. "He's probably thinking a hell of a lot that he's not saying, believe that."

"I'm sorry, Paige. He has to know that it's not what it looks like. Things are good between you two, and you would never do anything to jeopardize that. He knows that." Nina tried to comfort her.

Her words did nothing to stop the tears that were now falling from Paige's eyes. "I love him, Nina. Whenever the subject of Marlon comes up, we never seem to see eye-to-eye, so I didn't even mention it to him. That's why I didn't even tell him about the house. He's been telling me to just let Marlon have the house. Now, this . . ." Paige sniffed. She looked at the clock. "We better hurry before both of us are late."

"Don't worry, it'll work out," Nina said when they pulled up to her office building.

"Thanks, Nina. I'll be here at five-thirty to get you."

Sitting in the parking lot of the library where she worked, Paige took out her cell phone and looked at the pictures again. She still could not believe someone could take them and then send them to Quincy. She scrolled up and down, trying to see if she could locate where they originated. Her stomach churned as she thought about what Quincy had to be thinking. She wanted to call him, but decided to wait until they met for lunch.

There was no way she could work this morning. She called in and let them know she was taking a personal day. Paige needed to clear her head before she met with Quincy.

It was almost noon when he finally called her. "You ready?"

"Yes. Where do you wanna meet at?" she asked nervously.

"You want me to pick you up?"

"I'm not at work."

"Where are you?"

"I'm at home. Quincy—"

"I'll be there in twenty minutes," he said and hung the phone up.

It was sooner than that when she heard the doorbell ring. She walked over and opened the door.

He stood in the doorway, not saying anything, confusion mixed with anger in his face. He walked behind her, and they stood in the living room.

"You wanna tell me what's going on?"

"There's nothing going on, *Q*, I swear."

"That's not what it's looking like, Paige. I just told you a few days ago that if there's something you need to tell me, go ahead. You know you never have a reason to lie to me." Quincy stared at her.

"I know that, Quincy, and I've never lied to you about anything. I will admit that I didn't volunteer any information, but I never lied."

"So because you didn't tell me you were still seeing Marlon, that justifies it?"

"I'm not seeing Marlon."

"Now I'm beginning to wonder if there was some truth to what Kasey was saying." He glared at her.

Paige's nervousness now changed into rage. She could not believe that he even said that. "Oh, so now I'm a liar, and Kasey is the honest one?— Is that what you're saying?"

"I can see where she could think that you and Marlon were messing around with each other. You always say how you can't stand him and how he disgusts you, but you still chitchat and laugh on the phone in the middle of the night. And from the looks on the pictures, you don't look like the archenemies that you claim to be. I don't know what to believe. You say one thing and then act another way." Quincy folded his arms.

"So you don't trust me?"

"Have you given me a reason to trust you?"

"I haven't given you a reason not to trust me, Quincy. You're not even giving me a chance to explain what was going on in the pictures."

"It's clear what's going on. He's kissing you, you're smiling—no explanation needed."

Paige tried to fight back the tears, but they fell from her eyes. "If you already think that, then why did you come over here to talk then? You already think I'm in the wrong. You think that I'm cheating with Marlon, right? Your mind is already set on knowing that I'm going behind your back and getting with him. What did you want to discuss? You already have all the answers, Q. Let you tell it, you don't even have to ask if I'm fucking Marlon, because you already know. So what's the big discussion supposed to be about?"

"You're right, there's no need for further discussion. I'm outta here." He turned and slammed the door behind him.

Good riddance, she thought. *I don't need a man that has no confidence in me anyway. He didn't even give me the chance to explain what happened. I'm better off this way.* She walked over and sat on the sofa, hugging one of the throw pillows to her. As she cried, she realized that it was the one that Quincy would use to put his head on when he was watching television.

The faint scent of him made her cry harder as she realized that the best thing that had ever happened to her had just walked out the door.

"Paige, is everything all right?" Camille walked into Paige's bedroom.

Paige sat up and looked at her. She was such a pretty girl, looking just like her brother. "Well, Cam, things are a little rough for me right now."

"Anything I can do to help?" Camille sat on the side of the bed.

"You can go and pick Myla and Jade up for me." Paige sighed.

"That's it?"

"Yeah. Take them and hang out for a while until I get myself together. Go to the movies, maybe Chuck E. Cheese. What time is it?"

"Four o'clock. Tell me what's wrong—I can see you've been crying."

"Well, Quincy and I broke up," Paige told her.

"Why?" Camille looked shocked. "I like Quincy!"

"Because someone sent him a picture of me and Marlon at lunch the other day." Paige sighed and showed her the picture. "Now he thinks that I've been cheating on him."

"But this is how Marlon kissed me," Camille said. "He kissed me on the forehead when he says hello. When he says good-bye, he kissed my chin."

"I know that, but Quincy doesn't. And it doesn't matter, because he doesn't trust me. It's okay. I'll be fine," Paige told her. "Can you just get the girls and hang out with them?"

"Sure. That's no problem. Look, Paige, let me talk to Quincy. I can tell him—"

"No, you don't need to talk to him," Paige said.

"But, maybe if he understood, then you all can stay together. You love each other."

"It takes more than love, Camille. It also takes trust and belief in the person you're with. Without trust, no relationship can last."

"I understand. Oh, I almost forgot to tell you. I think I found a job too."

"Really? Where?"

"I'll let you know once I find out if it's gonna work out," Camille told her. "I'll get the girls, Paige." Camille stood up and started out the door. "And, trust me, you and Quincy will work out.

Chapter 19

"I hired a personal assistant," Taryn announced. The salon was closed and the girls were having their monthly staff meeting.

"'A personal assistant'? What for?" Yaya asked.

"Because I realize that I need one. With everything going on here at the salon and my freelance work, it makes sense to me. Also, my personal assistant will also be responsible for scheduling my appointments for my regular clients, so that pathetic excuse for a receptionist you hired won't have to be bothered."

"Wow! Maybe I need to hire a personal assistant." Monya laughed.

Unamused by their comments, Yaya stared at both of them. After the discovery that Celeste had made for her, Yaya felt obligated to keep her on staff. She had decided instead of firing the girl, to help transform her. After all, she was an image consultant.

"Celeste is going to improve; I'm personally gonna work with her and see to it," Yaya told them.

"You must have plenty of time on your hands," Taryn responded.

"Anyway, where did you find this personal assistant?" Yaya asked.

"At the catalog shoot the other day. She happened to be there watching, and next thing you know, she was right there helping. She's the bomb. We even talked about me training her for artistry." Taryn shrugged.

"Wow! That's good," Monya said. "When does she start?"

"Well, I was just waiting to tell you both about her. Unlike someone, I like to discuss things before making a decision. So, do either of you have a problem with me having a personal assistant?" Taryn looked from one to the other.

"Nope." Monya nodded. "I think it's a great idea."

"I don't care," Yaya told her. "As long as you pay her and not the salon. We only have salary for one receptionist, and now that we're hiring a new nail tech, the budget is going to be tighter."

"I don't have a problem paying her. Just know that she's working for me and not After Effex. I'll let her know she can start next week."

"Whatever." Yaya looked at her watch. "Well, I gotta go. I have a date with Jason tomorrow night, and I've got to get ready. *T*, can you fill my lashes in?"

"Yaya, why did you wait until the last minute? You know Lincoln is picking me up in a few minutes. Come on."

Yaya sat in Taryn's chair and closed her eyes, preparing herself to enjoy the pampering. Taryn had always had a gentle touch, and Yaya loved it.

"Can you do my brows too?"

"Yaya, I'm not gonna be here with you all night. Hold your head back. So . . . what's the deal with you and Jason now?"

"I gave him his space, and now he misses me, I guess," Yaya told her.

"So you all are officially back together?"

"*T*, we were never really broken up; we were just on a break."

"You said the break was over, when we opened the salon," Monya said.

"It was. I mean, we hooked up that night, and we still talk—"

"How many times have you 'hooked up' during the break?" Taryn interrupted.

Yaya opened her eyes.

Taryn quickly yelled, "Close 'em!"

"I mean, you know we hook up every so often."

"Yaya, you've been sleeping with him this entire time?" Taryn tugged at Yaya's lashes.

"A sister has needs; besides, it's not like he's not my boyfriend, come on."

"He's not—not if you're on a break; you're still screwing him without a commitment. You're asking to get hurt," Monya told her.

"Okay, hello, this is Jason—the man I'm going to marry." Yaya could not believe her girlfriends were saying this to her. They were acting as if she was out sleeping with some stranger she met at the club. "It's not like we do it all the time anyway."

"Only when he calls and wants to come through, huh?" Taryn asked.

"I didn't say that." Yaya didn't want to admit that she was right.

"You're giving him all the power, Yaya," Monya told her. "You're letting him control the direction of the relationship. You'd better start telling him no. He has it easy right now. He can go out and do what he wants and still come hit it when he wants to."

"That's not true. He's not going out and doing anything."

"If that's what you wanna believe, girlfriend. All I'm saying is that you need to clarify if Jason even wants to get back together for real, for real,"

Monya said. "He may honestly believe that you like things the way they are."

"He's using you."

"He's not using me. And while you're talking about me, what's up with you and Lincoln?—What do you call what you two are doing?"

"Lincoln and I are friends," Taryn answered.

"I think it's a tad bit more than that, *T*—You are all into him. You're going out, talking on the phone, he's coming over to the house."

"Which is what friends do!"

"But does he know how you feel? Have you asked him what's up?" Monya asked.

"He knows I'm feeling him. Why else would I be spending time with him? He knew that from day one." Taryn laughed.

"Yeah, we all knew you were feeling him from day one, Ms. Can't-Keep-My-Eyes-Off-Him!"

They laughed.

"So, Taryn, have you developed feelings for him? Does he have feelings for you? What's the deal? You're telling me I need to talk to Jason, but believe me, he knows I'm in love with him."

"Are you in love with Lincoln, *T*?" Monya asked.

The shop got eerily quiet.

Taryn pondered before she said, "Lincoln and I are friends—that's all that matters right now."

***

"Jason, can I ask you a question?" Yaya said as they drove to the restaurant the following night.

"Go ahead." He turned the radio down.

She tried to find the right words. "What is this that we're doing? I mean, where are we headed?"

"We're headed to the Pier to have dinner." He laughed.

"You know what I mean, Jason. You said you needed your space and I've respected that. I've also been obliging you those late nights when you come over to the crib and sleep with me. Is this all you want from me at this point, or are we going to go back to the way things were when we were together?"

Jason looked over at her. "Qianna, baby, you know how much we've been through. We've been together for a long time. I can't see myself with anyone else but you. The whole point of our giving each other space was so that we could attain some personal goals that we each wanted to achieve. You know I'm trying to make partner at work, and your business is successful right now. We are going to get back to the point where we were, soon. I keep telling you to take advantage of the time we're giving each other."

Yaya frowned, thinking while what he said sounded good, it didn't really answer her question. Not wanting to ruin the mood of the evening, she just sat back and said, "I can respect that, Jason."

"Great." He reached over and touched her thigh, causing tingles to rise inside her body.

She remained quiet for the remainder of the ride to the Pier.

Like the true gentleman he was, Jason opened the car door for her and held her hand as they walked inside. The elegant restaurant was one of her favorites. It was where they had come for their first date over three years ago.

She looked at their reflections as they waited in the lobby and thought they made the perfect couple. *Time will tell.*

"Mr. Taylor," Claudius, the maître d', greeted them, "so glad to see you again, sir. The rest of your party is already waiting."

Yaya looked over at Jason. "Rest of what party?"

"Just McDaniel's and his wife, that's all," he whispered, tucking a curl behind her ear. "You look so damn sexy in that dress. I know you got something special under there for me."

"Right this way, sir," Claudius told them.

Jason grabbed her by the hand and led her to the table where Jason's boss and his wife were seated.

"Jason." The older, handsome man stood. "Qianna, you're looking beautiful as usual. Wonderful to see you again. You remember my wife, Ellen?"

"Hello, Mr. McDaniels, Mrs. McDaniels." Qianna smiled at them. She waited as Jason pulled her chair out for her.

"What's with the formalities? You know it's Martin and Ellen." Martin smiled at her.

"My husband is right—you are absolutely stunning," Ellen told her. "I was telling my daughter about you the other day."

"Jason tells us you've opened quite the establishment, young lady," Martin said, after they had ordered their meals.

Yaya was shocked that Jason had even talked about her. "Yes, sir." She nodded. "It's doing quite well."

"So, tell me about it, my dear," Ellen said.

Yaya told them of the salon and the services they offered and the goals they had for the future.

By the time dinner arrived, she realized she had monopolized the entire conversation. "I'm sorry. I got a little carried away."

"Nonsense," Ellen said. "I think it's wonderful. You're beautiful, talented, smart, and successful—everything a man could possibly want in a woman. If Jason didn't already have you on his arms, I would be on my phone right now calling one of my nephews."

"I don't think so. I claimed this woman as my soul mate years ago, and that's not gonna change."

Yaya looked at Jason to see if he was sincere in what he was saying.

He put his hand on the back of her neck and rubbed it lightly.

"It's so nice to see two successful young people. You two are the picture of perfection. Jason, I have to admit, you have brought so much to the company, including Qianna. I see nothing but great things in the future for both of you."

"Thank you, sir." Jason smiled and pulled Yaya closer to him.

"This has certainly been a pleasure tonight," Martin told them, after they had finished dessert.

"I look forward to seeing you both at the company retreat in a few weeks. It's being held at the Poconos." Ellen nodded at them.

"I would love to attend, but it's only for junior and senior partners, Ellen." Jason laughed.

"I believe you'll be included in the invites this time, Jason." Martin winked. "I'll see you bright and early Monday morning."

"Yes, sir." Jason stood and shook his hand and then hugged Ellen. Yaya did the same.

They walked into the parking lot and said their good-byes.

"They are really nice," she said as they walked to the car.

Jason didn't respond.

She looked over at him to see if he heard her.

He was staring at her.

She stopped and turned to him. "What?"

"You are one-of-a-kind, you know that?" He shook his head as he faced her.

Her heart began pounding. She tried to think of what she had done wrong. "What are you talking about?"

He pulled her to him, crushing his mouth on hers and kissing her like he had never done before. It was filled with so much emotion that she felt lightheaded.

They stood kissing each other for what seemed like hours.

She laughed. "Where did that come from?"

"It's been there the entire time, baby."

The look in his eyes was one she had been waiting to see for weeks; she knew that he once again loved her.

"I am so proud of you. I am so amazed by you. You are my ideal woman."

"Jason, you're tripping." She tried to think of how many drinks he had during dinner; he had never been this verbal about his feelings. "Are you okay to drive?"

"I'm fine, Yaya. Come on, I just wanna get home so I can see what's under that dress." He pulled her toward the car.

They'd barely made it through the door when he reached for the zipper of her dress.

"Golly, Jason, let me at least get in the house first." She giggled.

Once inside, she paused long enough to let him unzip it. It fell to the floor, and she stepped out of it.

Just as he predicted, she had on a sexy black lace and embroidered corset she'd ordered from Victoria's Secret. "That's what I've been waiting all night to see," he whispered.

She turned her back to him, so he could remove it.

He kissed the back of her shoulders as he unhooked it. His lips then formed a trail down to the small of her back, until he reached the lace panties she wore.

Heat radiated through her body, and her nipples hardened. She moaned, losing her breath with each touch.

He took her by the hand and led her up the steps. "Come on."

When they entered her bedroom, he removed his shirt.

She kissed his shoulder, licking his collarbone, her arms clasped around his waist.

He pulled her toward the bathroom and turned on the shower. Steam instantly surrounded them.

She reached and unfastened his pants as he sucked her neck. Yaya didn't care about her hair or make-up as they stepped inside the shower. She welcomed the hot water on her body, standing directly under the cascade.

Jason reached and grabbed the bottle of Jamaican Punch and poured a small amount onto the loofah. He proceeded to gently bathe her, taking time to stimulate her most sensual areas. Her knees felt weak as he kneeled between her legs and teased her with his tongue.

She grabbed his head with one hand and the rail of the shower with the other, to brace herself. "Jason," she moaned, "you've gotta stop."

He looked up at her and smiled.

She reached and took the sponge from him, now taking her turn to bathe him. She turned his back to her, sensually kissing his back as she bathed it.

When she was done, he turned to face her.

She ran the textured object along his torso, pausing right above his navel. Then she kneeled before him and took him into her mouth, teasing him with her tongue, pleasuring him.

He grabbed her wet hair and pulled it.

The pain aroused her even more, and when she heard her name escape from his mouth, she knew he could take no more.

She stood, and he kissed her again.

He stopped the water, and they stepped out. He grabbed a towel and wrapped it around his waist then lifted her wet body into his arms and carried her to her bed.

"Jason, I'm still wet."

"I know. I want you to stay that way." He removed his towel and then climbed onto the bed.

She closed her eyes and prepared herself for the lovemaking she knew he had in store for her.

He entered her, gently at first, then faster and harder.

She wrapped her legs around his body, wanting to feel all of him. She wanted him to feel how much she wanted him, how much she loved and needed him. Her hips rotated, and she thrust faster and faster each time he penetrated. She couldn't get enough of him.

"Yaya," he cried out.

"Yes, baby," she whispered, biting his neck.

He tried to answer but couldn't.

She arched her back and tightened herself, making sure he felt every ounce of her climax. She panted and fell back on the bed. The smell of sweat and the scented bath oil filled her nose.

"Oh, God!" Jason rolled off her.

"What?"

"That was the best sex I've ever had in my life." He laughed.

"It was all right." She smiled, knowing that she had outdone herself.

He went back into the bathroom.

She climbed under the covers.

He climbed back into bed with her, and she snuggled next to his warm body.

Feeling better than she had in months, Yaya fell into a deep slumber.

Hours later, she rolled over to find that she was all alone.

Chapter 20

Paige slowly got out of her car and walked up to Meeko's door. It had taken everything within her to make it over here. She and Quincy had only been apart three days, but it felt like a lifetime. Having brunch with her mother, aunts, and cousins was the last thing she felt like doing. She knew there was no way she could get out of attending, though. Camille and Myla had already arrived thirty minutes earlier, and her mother had called twice, asking where she was.

"About time," Meeko said, opening the door. She leaned over and gave Paige a kiss on the cheek. Paige frowned when she noticed Meeko's apron. "What in the world?—I know you aren't cooking."

"Girl, naw. It's cute though, huh? And it matches my outfit." Meeko struck a model pose, causing Paige to laugh. "I noticed that Oprah wears an apron when she entertains, for an added effect, even though we all know she doesn't cook."

"Okay, Oprah."

"Wait, wait, wait. I gotta go outside and check out the new ride. I just knew you would've driven over here; now I can see it."

Meeko brushed past her, and they walked into the circular driveway in front of the house, where Paige had parked her new car behind what was now Camille's jeep.

"This is the bomb, girl. I am so happy for you. I love this color. It's fly!" Meeko said, admiring the car.

The excitement Paige once held for her new vehicle was diminished by the sadness she was feeling.

It didn't take Meeko long to notice. "What's wrong?"

"Everything—I called myself making a wise decision, and it turned out to be a bad one." Paige sighed. She leaned against the car and told Meeko what happened between her and Quincy days before.

"So have you spoken to him at all?" Meeko put her arms around Paige. "Why are you just now telling me all of this? Why didn't you call when this all happened?"

"I don't know. I know you're busy with Isaiah and Stanley, besides you were hosting this brunch."

"Girl, please . . . you're the closest thing I have to a sister, and you know anything you're going through, I'm going through with you. I can't believe this. I still don't know where the picture could've come from." Meeko shook her head.

"I don't know. He never even told me, and I tried to find where it originated from."

"Have you talked to Marlon? Did he see the picture?"

"'Marlon'? No. I haven't seen or heard from him since that day. If someone did send him the picture, he hasn't said anything to me about it."

"This is crazy. Look, don't worry. This will all blow over, and you and Quincy will be back together in no time, you two are meant to be."

"I don't even know if I want to be with him, Meeko. Not after this. He didn't even give me a chance to explain what happened. He even had the nerve to tell me that maybe Kasey was right when she said Marlon and I had been creeping out together."

"That was just him talking in anger, you know how that is. Come on, let's go inside. Everyone else is already here."

"Don't tell me Celeste is here." Paige groaned.

"Girl, and she is in such a good mood, you'd think she finally got a man or something." Meeko put her arm around Paige as they walked back to the house.

From the looks of the spread, Meeko had learned a lot from Oprah. Her Southern-style seafood brunch was to die for. She hadn't forgotten anything, from the fried catfish and stewed tomatoes to the seafood omelets and Belgian waffles. The food was delicious, right down to the fresh-squeezed lemonade.

Paige made it a point to stay clear of Celeste and her mother, and was fairly quiet, speaking and commenting only when spoken directly to.

"So, did Celeste tell you about her new part-time job?" Aunt Gayle volunteered. "She's working as an image consultant."

"'Image consultant'?" Meeko, Paige, and Nina all said at the same time.

Camille began laughing so hard, she nearly choked.

"Yes, she is," Aunt Gayle snapped at them. "You three aren't the only ones who can have nice job titles."

"That's wonderful, Celeste," Paige's mother said. "Where are you working?"

Celeste looked like she wanted to run away. "It's just a part-time job, Mama. It's not that great."

"Don't be embarrassed, Celeste. Tell them about your job," Aunt Gayle said. "I'm proud of you."

Paige, you're not perfect, and not everyone looks at you through rose-colored glasses. Your world is slowly crumbling down around you. Look at it—you had a man for seven years and he still ain't marry you, he married the woman across the street that treated him like a man. Now, she's carrying his son—Another man you had but couldn't keep."

Paige flinched from the sting of Celeste's hateful words.

"Celeste," Meeko said in a warning voice.

"Then you got with Quincy and thought you had hit the cream of the crop, until he saw you for himself, who you really were, and now, once again, you're back to square one. I guess you're no different than me, huh, Paige? Because right now, you ain't got a man either." Celeste laughed cynically.

Paige thought she was dreaming. She had never hit someone so hard and so fast in her life. Her fist connected to Celeste's mouth, and blood came pouring out. She reached out and grabbed a handful of her hair and yanked her to the ground, taking all the frustration, hurt, and anger out on her cousin.

She could hear her mother screaming her name. The room came to utter chaos.

She closed her eyes and continued punching Celeste, thinking that somehow, just maybe, she could knock some sense into her.

It was Camille who was finally able to get a grip on Paige and pull her off.

Paige huffed and puffed as she fixed her shirt, which was now twisted.

Camille led her out the front door and held her tight.

Now, an emotional wreck, Paige cried in her arms.

Nina came out and joined them, and the three embraced in a group hug.

When she got herself together enough to look up, Paige saw that they were crying also. "What the hell is wrong with y'all?" She wiped the tears from her face.

Camille looked over at Nina and smiled. "We're sad because you got to beat her up and we didn't."

As hard as she had just cried, Paige now laughed even harder.

Nina said, "You know you're in big trouble, right?"

"*Big* ain't even the word," Paige said.

"I can't believe this is the second fight I've had to break up that involved you," Camille reminded her. "First, you kick Lucille's ass, and now Celeste's. You catch Kasey on the right day, and you'll be three for three."

The door opened and Meeko walked out. "I know like hell you wenches ain't out here giggling about this. Paige, you broke that girl's glasses. She's in there moaning and groaning so bad, we may have to take her to the hospital, and you're out here laughing like it's a joke."

They looked at each other and began laughing even harder than before.

Meeko could no longer hold a straight face. "You shoulda seen the look on her face, when you bust her in the mouth." She giggled. "Her eyes liked to have jumped out her head!"

"I'm just glad the kids were upstairs in the theater room. That would've been awful for them to see." Paige sighed. "I feel bad."

Laughter erupted again.

"Seriously, I've got to go back in and apologize to my mother."

"I don't think now is the right time," Meeko said. "They are in there fanning all over Celeste. She needs someone to 'consult her image' right about now."

"I can't believe her," Nina commented.

"How did she know that you and Quincy broke up?" Camille asked. "I guess your mom told her."

"My mother doesn't even know we broke up. I didn't mention anything to her about it. I was gonna wait and see how everything played itself out and then tell her once I knew for sure we were over."

Celeste's words began to replay in Paige's head. "*He saw for himself how you really are.*" Paige knew that she had something to do with Quincy getting that picture. "She set me up."

"You think she's the one?" Meeko asked.

"I think she and Kasey probably schemed together," Nina added.

"I say you go in there and ask her," Camille said.

"No, I'm leaving, but you'd better believe— payback is a mutha, and Celeste is gonna get hers."

Chapter 21

"You want me to back everything up on a disc in case something happens, like—God forbid—the computer crashes?"

"I think that's a great idea."

"At least, that way you'll still have copies of your client master list if you are traveling. They have the cutest jump drives now that fit right on your keychain. If you're doing an event in L.A. and you need a model at the last minute, you can go right to the hotel computer, pop it into the drive, and there you have the master list."

"Girl, you are the bomb! I don't know what I'd do without you and today's your first day."

Yaya stood outside Taryn's office and listened. *She must be talking to her new personal assistant.* She entered her own office.

She was worn out, physically and emotionally. After everything that happened Saturday night, Jason was back to playing this cat-and-mouse game. He was really tripping, and she was irritated.

Then, to top things off, Quincy seemed to be a walking emotional wreck. She had never seen her brother so let down. If she didn't know any better, she'd think that having him find out about Paige cheating with Marlon was a bad thing.

She put her things away and walked back into the salon. "Where's Celeste?" She looked over at Monya, who had finished one client and was already working on another one.

"Remember she said something about having to take her mom to the doctor or something this week?"

"That's right." She sat at the receptionist desk. There were sticky pads all over with half-written messages. Some were even for her. *I know we gave this girl a message book to keep messages in and told her she could put them in our individual mailboxes on the office doors.*

"Hey, Yaya," Taryn said. "You remember Camille, right?"

Yaya turned to see the pretty girl standing beside Taryn. She was sharply dressed in white linen pants and a black halter-top. Yaya actually owned a pair of the same Kenneth Cole black sandals the girl had on her feet.

"Oh, yes, I remember her. How are you?"

"I'm great. It's nice seeing you again." Camille smiled.

"Camille is my new personal assistant, Yaya." Taryn smiled.

"I'm sure you'll do a fine job, Camille. Feel free to ask for help in any way." Yaya turned to Taryn. "Can I see you in the back for a minute?"

"Sure. Camille, we'll be right back." Taryn followed Yaya to the back.

"What the hell are you doing? You know that girl is Paige's ex-boyfriend's sister! She lives with Paige."

"What?" Taryn frowned. "And?"

"I don't need any drama around here. Okay, you know Paige and Quincy broke up," Yaya whispered.

"And?" Taryn continued to stare at her like she was speaking a foreign language.

"If she's working here, that means Paige is gonna stop by or come visit."

"She does that anyway, Yaya; she's my regular client." Taryn sighed. "Look, I'm sure that Quincy and Paige won't be running into each other here at the salon. He only comes by here like once a week at the most. And if she does happen to be here, then I believe they are adult enough to remain civil to one another."

"But what if Quincy begins dating someone else who becomes a client, won't that cause problems?" Yaya asked. "Then Camille will go back and tell Paige about Quincy's new girlfriend."

"Yaya, you sound like you're in the sixth grade. Here at this salon, we're all about business. And, remember, Camille is my personal assistant—I'm paying her, not After Effex."

They walked back into the salon.

"Thanks for calling After Effex, where before and after are never the same.

"She's not available at the moment. Is there something I can help you with this morning?" Camille placed her hand over the phone. "Monya is sorta busy, and the phone was ringing, so I just answered it. Is that okay?"

"That's great." Taryn smiled at Camille and winked at Yaya. "Tell you what—why don't you hang out here and cover the phones since Celeste isn't coming in?"

"'Celeste'?" Camille had a strange look on her face.

"Yes. Celeste is our receptionist. She hasn't made it in yet," Yaya answered. "You don't have to answer the phones; I know that's not what you're being paid to do."

"Uh, I don't have a problem covering the phones. That's cool." Camille shrugged and sat down.

Within minutes, it was as if she was a pro who had been working there for years.

"Yaya, you have some messages," Camille told her later that afternoon, as she was about to leave. "I was about to put them in the inbox hanging on your office door. I'll see you all tomorrow."

"Bye, Camille. Thanks for everything!" Taryn waved.

"Have a good evening," Monya called to her.

"Thanks, Camille."

"I like her," Monya announced.

"Me too. That's why I hired her."

"Whatever." Yaya flipped through the neatly written messages that had actual time and dates written on them. She stopped when she came to one from Diesel. She became excited, and rushed to call her long-time buddy, who was a radio personality and party promoter.

"What's up, Miss Q?" he greeted her.

"My man, Diesel, what the hell is going on?" She laughed.

"Yo, I got a job for you. It's a big one!"

"You know I'm down for it. What's going on?"

"I need you to meet me in D.C. next weekend, and bring me two of your hottest girls!"

"Next weekend?" Yaya looked on her calendar: She had a face to do for a girl's engagement photos. "Hold on, let me check something. Don't hang up. *T*, can you cover for me next Saturday at two? I'm supposed to do a face for some engagement pictures, it's not that hard. The girl is really cute."

Taryn looked over at her. "Let me get Camille to check my schedule, and I'll let you know."

"You're trying to be funny, *T*. Come on, Diesel wants me to fly to D.C. for a gig."

"Oh, goodness, Yaya . . . you and Diesel, I swear . . ." She sighed. "Fine, but you owe me."

"Thanks, *T*. You're the best!" Yaya ran back into her office and told him. "It's a done deal. I can come. So what do you need?"

"Two of your hottest chicks, and I mean, the baddest chicks you've ever worked with—I don't care where you have to fly them from—money is no object."

"This is all-expenses-paid, right?"

"No doubt. It's gonna be a two-day trip. Fly in Saturday and fly out Sunday. Anything before or after that is on you. Yaya, I'm depending on you because this shit is about to be off the chain."

"I know it is," Yaya told him. She mentally began going through her top clients. She had so many to choose from. She also knew that any party Diesel threw, there were gonna be some ballers there, and she couldn't bring any chicken-heads with her who would be star-struck.

The guest list for the last party she did for Diesel included Larenz Tate, Tyrese, Chris Webber, Chauncey Billups, Ben and Rasheed Wallace, just to name a few.

She was almost star-struck herself, but remained focused as she transformed six of the finest girls she worked with into zoo animals in bikinis. Once painted, they climbed into cages, where they danced the night away. It was a great event.

"What exactly are you thinking about, Diesel?"

"You know I can't tell you that until you get here. Just bring the two chicks . . . make one light and one dark—yeah, that's gonna be hot. Oh, and don't forget your make-up."

"Diesel, you know me and my girls don't do the freaky stuff, right?"

"Girl, you know I respect you more than that. Call me and let me know what time you all will be arriving, so I can have a car waiting."

"Will do." Yaya hung up the phone. She decided that her best bets would be Sophia and Gabrielle. Sophia was Haitian by birth and lived in Miami. She had the darkest, most beautiful complexion Yaya had ever worked with. Gabrielle was her Puerto Rican party girl, living in Dallas. Her body was banging enough to make J-Lo bow down.

She called both girls to check their availability and see if they were down for the trip. She knew that both of them were cool enough to party with, but sophisticated enough to act like ladies. Both were flattered to be considered and agreed to the job.

"What do you and Diesel have going on?" Monya asked.

"You know I never know until I get there." Yaya laughed. "Whatever it is, it will be memorable. You should tag along. He said he needs two girls, but I'm sure he'll take three."

"I don't think so." Monya laughed. "Those days of my life are long gone."

"Please . . . you act like you're old—I can't believe Celeste didn't show up. I hope everything's okay."

"Maybe you should call," Taryn told her.

"Yeah, I guess I should." Yaya sighed.

Just as she was about to dial the number, Quincy pulled in front of the shop.

She ran out to greet her brother. "Hey, *Q*!" She gave him a hug.

"What's up, Yaya," he said, not sounding himself.

She knew he would still be hurting behind Paige, but not like this. His clothes seemed to be rumpled and of all things; he needed a haircut.

"You look terrible, *Q*," she told him.

"Gee, thanks. I feel worse, believe that. Man, I'm tired as hell, and I just can't get myself together."

"Don't get like this, *Q*. You know everything is gonna work out; they always do. You just gotta get over that girl, I'm telling you. She's not even worth you stressing about her."

"Then how come I don't feel that way, Yaya? You know me better than anyone. When I'm done with someone, I'm done. Every relationship I've been in that didn't work out, I knew there was a reason behind it, and I was cool with it.

"This one is different, I know it. I just can't figure this out.

It's crazy because I don't even know where the damn picture came from or even who took it. It's like it appeared out of nowhere."

Yaya nodded as her brother talked. She was glad that she and Celeste decided to send it from a pre-paid phone that they'd bought from a guy in the shop. Once they sent the picture, they threw the phone away.

"I don't know, *Q*, everything done in the dark comes to light. Just be glad you found out now and not later. Think about if you really had asked her to marry you—better yet, you had married her."

"That sounds good and all, but it doesn't make me feel better, or love her any less."

"Q, don't be stupid. How could you say that about a girl that was cheating on you in broad daylight with her ex-boyfriend who's married? What does that say about her? If she really loved you, would she have done that?" Yaya could not believe he was standing here still saying he loved this girl. Paige had to have put a root or some type of spell on him.

"I was thinking, maybe he sent the picture."

"Who?"

"Marlon. Maybe he did it to be funny." Quincy leaned on the edge of his car and looked deep in thought.

Yaya folded her arms. "Why would Marlon send it?"

"To cause us to break up. I know he's still trying to get her back. He still loves her. I've heard him say it myself."

"Quincy, you're trying to make sense out of nonsense. He doesn't have to break you all up. They're together, even though he's married. Just let it go, Q. Move on. You've got enough stress with opening the new shop and everything else. It's her loss."

"Then why do I feel like I'm the one that lost everything?"

Suddenly, his attention turned to a jeep that pulled beside his.

The door opened. Camille got out, followed by the cute little girl Yaya remembered meeting at the grand opening.

She ran over and hopped into Quincy's arms. "Hi, Mr. Quincy." The little girl grinned.

"Hey, Ms. Myla." He kissed her on the cheek.

He let Camille know that everything was okay, and she went into the salon.

"Guess what?"

"What?" Quincy put the little girl down and tugged on one of her ponytails.

"I'm gonna play soccer."

"'Soccer'?—that's for boys."

"No, it's not!"

"Girls are supposed to be cheerleaders."

"I'm going to be one of those too," she said. "But I'm going to play soccer this summer and then be a cheerleader for football season."

"You sound like you're gonna be pretty busy, Ms. Myla."

"Not too busy to go for a ride on your bike." Her eyes widened, and she grinned, showing her dimples. "We can go after my games, okay?"

"Myla, come on, let's go," Camille called, when she came out the door.

"What's up, Camille?" He gave her a half-smile. "I keep forgetting Paige gave you the jeep."

"And I'm loving it too! Come on, Myla, we gotta go."

"Okay, bye, Mr. Quincy. I'll see you later." Myla hugged him tight. "Are you coming over to our house tonight?"

Quincy leaned over and looked into her eyes.

Yaya could see the love her brother had for the little girl.

"I have to work, Myla, but I promise I will be at your first game."

"I know you will." Myla ran and jumped into the jeep.

They all waved, as Camille and Myla drove off.

"Paige got another car?" Yaya asked.

"Yeah. She copped the Benz from Titus." Quincy nodded. "It's a nice ride."

"What? Stop playing!" Yaya snapped. "I wanted that car! I told Titus."

"You didn't need that car; you already have two cars."

"And you have four! I can't believe she got that car. How could she pay for it? Doesn't she work at the library making like ten dollars an hour?"

"What?" He frowned. "Paige is the head librarian. She has a master's degree. She makes about sixty thousand a year."

Yaya was now confused. She distinctly remembered Celeste telling her that Paige barely could pay her bills every month and lived for free in their cousin's townhouse. Celeste made it clear that Paige was a golddigger, if there ever was one.

"Then why doesn't she pay rent?"

"What makes you think she doesn't pay rent? She pays a mortgage each month."

"That's her cousin's place, isn't it?"

"Yeah, but Page is buying it from her. Meeko and Stan hold the mortgage because it's already paid for. She pays them directly . . . like Uncle Fred did for me before he gave me the building."

"Oh," was all she could say.

Quincy explaining all of this to her still didn't change the fact that she had been cheating with her ex. And to her, that was unforgivable.

Chapter 22

"We saw Mr. Quincy today," Myla said while they ate dinner. Paige almost choked on the chicken she was eating. "Saw him where?" "We went to Aunt Cam's job. He was standing outside talking to a pretty lady."

"Oh, really? That's nice," Paige said, nonchalantly. *Didn't take him long to move on. He was probably already cheating, which is why he tripped about that stupid picture.*

"He says he's coming to my first soccer game. I like Mr. Quincy."

"Eat those peas," Paige told her.

Camille came in and sat at the table. She tried to resist, but had to ask, "You saw Quincy today?"

"Yeah. I was gonna tell you, but I guess someone beat me to the punch."

Camille looked across the table at her niece.

Myla shrugged. "I didn't know it was a secret."

"You can't hold water, can you?" Camille shook her head.

"We did see him this afternoon."

"She told me he was with a pretty girl."

Again, Camille gave Myla a threatening look.

"He was," Myla said, pretending to concentrate on her peas.

"He was with his sister!" Camille laughed.

"His sister is pretty." Myla nodded. "She has really long eyelashes."

"They're fake," Camille told her. "I know how to put them on. You want me to do yours?"

Myla started looking excited.

"No!" Paige announced to both of them. "You're not getting any eyelashes, and you're not putting any on her. That's her problem now—she thinks she's grown."

"I was just kidding, Paige. Myla, you can't get eyelashes until you're ten."

"Don't play with me." Paige tried not to smile. "So where did you see him?"

"You mean Barbara Walters, Junior here didn't tell you?"

"She said you were at your job, which by the way you still haven't told me about."

"Well, you are now looking at Taryn Owens' personal assistant," Camille said with pride.

"You're working for Taryn at the shop?" Paige wasn't at all impressed.

"Well . . . not at the shop. I pretty much work wherever she needs me—from home, the shop—I get to go with her when she travels sometimes. I think it's going to be cool; plus the pay is more than I expected. She's so talented and smart. I know I'm gonna learn so much from her," Camille said without taking a breath.

"And how did all of this come about?"

Camille went on to tell her how she ran into Taryn at what she thought was about to be a fashion show, but turned out to be a fashion shoot.

"So what is she gonna do when you go back to school in the fall?"

The smile faded from Camille's face. "I don't know. I hadn't even thought about that. All I know is this is the opportunity of a lifetime, Paige, and I'm gonna take advantage of it."

"And I think you should. But school has got to be a priority too. Think about it. The only reason I'm able to move ahead when your brother and I split up is because I had my education to fall back on. You've got your entire life ahead of you, and more opportunities are gonna come; this is just one of many."

"I know." Camille sighed. "Oh my goodness! I know what I forgot to tell you—guess who the receptionist at the salon is?"

"Who?" Paige asked.

"Celeste!"

"Tell me you're lying." Paige sat back in her chair.

"No. She didn't show up for work today either. She must still be recuperating from the beating you gave her." Camille laughed.

Paige nodded toward Myla. "Not right now."

"Oh, well, yeah, Yaya was saying how she didn't even call or anything."

"She was probably with Aunt Gayle. You know her dialysis started today. I called Mama, but they were at the hospital, and she couldn't talk." Paige stood up and picked her plate up off the table. "Eat those peas, Myla."

"I was thinking, what if Celeste showed Yaya the picture and that's how Quincy got it?"

Paige began to wonder the same thing. If Celeste was somehow working at the shop, she had probably given Yaya more than an earful of lies and half-truths. "That may be possible. Myla, go throw your plate away. You're playing in your food, and that's nasty. And no, you can't have ice-cream."

"Awww, Mom." Myla got up from the table and walked into the kitchen.

Once she was gone, Paige sat back down.

Camille continued, "Then there's the fact that I looked at the appointment book and saw that Kasey has been coming in there to get her nails done too. I can't believe Monya or Taryn would even touch her."

"This is crazy. You should talk to Quincy, really. I don't even know if he knows she works there. Monya says the girl barely comes to work, and when she does, she's always in Yaya's office talking about something—my guess is that it's you."

"I'm not talking to Quincy. Even if this is the case, he made the assumption without even giving me the chance to explain. He believed who he wanted to believe, and that wasn't me—that shows me right there that he doesn't trust me."

Paige cleaned the kitchen and put away the food and then walked upstairs to her bedroom. Sitting on the side of her bed, she looked over at the clock and noticed it was still fairly early.

She went back downstairs and grabbed her keys. "Camille!"

"Yeah!" Camille yelled back.

"I'm going out for a while. I'll be back later!"

"Where are you going, Mommy?" Myla stood at the top of the steps.

"I'll be back," Paige said, walking out the door.

She got into her car and sat back, indulging herself in the lavishness of the leather seats. She started the engine and began driving, not having a set destination.

For hours, she drove around aimlessly, just thinking and listening to music. When the car finally stopped, she was parked in front of After Effex. The parking lot was empty, and the lights were off. Even the barbershop was closed.

Why the hell am I over here? She put the car in reverse and was about to back up, when a car pulled beside hers. She turned to see Yaya staring at her.

She put the car back into park and remained still.

Yaya opened the car door and stepped out, walking over to Paige.

Paige rolled the window down.

"What's up?" Yaya asked, her voice full of attitude.

"I don't know. I guess I rode over here to find that out myself."

"What do you mean by that?"

"I think we need to talk—You got a few minutes?" Paige opened her door and got out.

"I got a second."

"I'm beginning to think—no, let me correct that—I know that you seem to have a problem with me. I just need to know why?" Paige inhaled and exhaled slowly.

Yaya blinked several times.

Paige noticed the eyelashes that Myla and Camille were speaking of earlier. *I have to admit, they do look nice. I wouldn't mind having some myself—girl, stop tripping and concentrate on the subject at hand.*

"I don't have a problem with you at all, Paige. Whatever is going on between you and my brother is between you and my brother. It's none of my business."

Paige took a chance at asking, "Was it your business when you sent that picture to his phone that Celeste sent you?"

"I didn't have anything to do with the picture. I will tell you this—I think that what you did to Quincy was dirty as hell, and I don't appreciate it one bit. My brother cared a lot about you, and not only that, he cared for your daughter. A lot of brothers out here wouldn't do that—don't blame me because you messed it up because you couldn't leave your baby daddy alone."

"Is that what you think happened? Or was that what Celeste told you? I know my cousin very well—she's a manipulator, and she's very good at what she does. She has a way of twisting and turning things to make people look a certain way, and she also has a way of turning situations into her favor. She makes people feel sorry for her—they give her money, they give her jobs. I mean, that's just her; she's been like that her entire life."

"What does that have to do with me?" Yaya raised her eyebrows.

"Consider this a warning."

"A warning for what? I know you're not threatening me. I told you I didn't have anything to do with you and Quincy; none of this is my fault."

"No, there's no need to feel threatened. This isn't even about Quincy and I; it's about you and your employee. You see, I'm used to Celeste turning on me, but there's going to come a time when she's going to turn on you and you're going to find yourself looking crazy. I advise you to watch your back and the ones around you, because she doesn't care who she hurts in the process."

With that, Paige got back into her car and drove off. She looked in her rearview mirror and saw Yaya still standing and watching her.

Chapter 23

"I've looked everywhere! It's not at home, it's not here!" Yaya yelled from the storage room.

"I know Taryn took it!"

"She said she didn't have it," Monya replied.

"Celeste just called and asked her."

"She's lying. I know she probably grabbed mine thinking it was hers!" Yaya continued to look for the set of brushes that was usually in her make-up kit.

Packed and all set to leave for the airport, she did a double-check of her bags and saw that her brushes were missing. She stopped by the salon, hoping they were there, but she was wrong.

"What time does your flight leave?" Monya asked.

"Six-thirty!"

"It's only two o'clock, Yaya. Chill out!"

"You know everything has to be perfect for this trip, girl. Don't even try it," Yaya told her.

"Celeste, can you call Taryn again for me?" Yaya asked.

Her cell began ringing. It was Jason. "Yeah."

"'*Yeah*'—what kind of way is that to answer your phone?"

"I knew it was you, Jason. What's up?—I'm kinda busy right now."

"I'm calling to make sure you'll be ready to leave in the morning," he said.

"Ready for what?"

"The retreat—the one for my job. We're going to the Poconos, babe, remember?"

She didn't remember. Well, she did, but he hadn't said anything to her about it the two times they had spoken since that night.

"Jason, I can't go to the Poconos with you. I'm sorry, but I am flying out of town to work tonight."

"Qianna, do not play with me. You know how important this weekend is to me. Stop tripping!"

"I'm not tripping and I'm not playing! I'm dead serious. I have a flight leaving out this evening, and I'll be gone for two days. I gotta go." She closed the phone and put it on the shelf. She knew he was pissed, but she didn't care. The only thing that mattered was that she find those brushes and get ready for the weekend.

"Yaya, you have a call," Celeste said.

"Take a message! You know I'm trying to get outta here, Celeste, damn!" *That girl has got to be the most incompetent receptionist in the world. She'd better be glad her mother was ill, or she would definitely be fired.*

"He says it's an emergency."

Yaya rushed to the phone, thinking it may have been Quincy calling about something. "Hello," she panted.

"Hey, what's up, Yaya. It's Fitz."

"Man, I thought something was wrong. Celeste said it was an emergency."

"It is—do you know where Taryn is?"

"She is actually on a shoot for a hair book this afternoon."

"You know what time she'll be done?"

"Probably around eleven tonight. Those shoots last a while—What's going on?"

"I just needed her help, that's all. Listen, you think you can help me?"

Yaya frowned. "Help you with what?—I don't have any money!"

"Nothing like that, Yaya. Don't even insult me like that. You know how hard I work. Look, can you just grab your make-up stuff and meet me somewhere. It won't take that long, I promise."

"Meet you where?" she asked, still confused.

"Come on, I need a favor. You know I would never ask *you* of all people for a favor."

"I still don't know what the favor is, besides, Fitz, I have a plane to catch in a couple of hours, and I'm still not packed."

"Yaya, can you please come and meet me? I swear, I will never ask you for anything else as long as I live."

She hesitated, hearing the seriousness in his voice. "Fine. Tell me where, so I can hurry and get back."

She wrote down the directions he gave her.

Just as she was about to walk out, Celeste stopped her. "Um, are you coming back before you go to the airport?"

"I doubt if I'll have time."

"Well, um, I wanted to ask you if I can have my check early or maybe get an advance," Celeste said, sheepishly.

"Celeste, you've barely been to work these past two weeks."

"I know, but you know my mother's been ill, and I was there for her," Celeste said with tears in her eyes. "I'm the only one who's there to take care of her.

Yaya took a deep breath. "Celeste, I can't give you an advance or pay you for time you haven't worked. Taryn and Monya wouldn't even allow me to do that. It's just not in our budget right now, especially when we just hired the new nail techs."

Celeste whined, "I don't see how Taryn should have a problem with it, when she has her own personal flunkie around here."

"Camille's paycheck comes from Taryn not After Effex," Yaya said, wondering why she was even having this discussion.

"I'm my mother's only source of income, Yaya; I don't know what else to do." Celeste began crying.

Yaya immediately felt sorry for the girl. She reached into her purse and took out her checkbook. She wrote her a check for two hundred dollars out of her personal account and passed it to her. "Don't say anything to anyone about this."

"I won't, I promise." Celeste wiped her face.

Yaya rushed out and got into her car. She reached into her pocket to get the directions out, but realized she left them right on her desk. She didn't know Fitz's number, so she couldn't call him either.

"Dammit," she said as she focused and tried to recall what he said. She paused and closed her eyes and then as if by some sort of mental telepathy, she could hear his voice in her head instructing her. It was scary.

She followed them, and when she looked up, sure enough, she realized she was on Dickens Ct., exactly where she was supposed to be. She didn't know what the house number was, so she just made the turn.

Without fail, in the driveway of the biggest house in the center of the court was a burgundy Honda Accord station wagon. She pulled behind it and stepped out of her car.

The house was huge, sitting on what seemed to be ten acres of perfectly cut grass. It was her dream house—a two-story, brick mansion, complete with white columns and a fountain in front.

She walked up to the door. Just as she was about to ring the bell, the door opened.

Fitz stood in the doorway, smiling. "Thanks. This means a lot to me."

"I still don't know why I'm her."

"Come in and I'll explain it to you."

She stepped inside and took in the opulence of the place. The brightness of the skylights welcomed her into the foyer. "Wow, this place is amazing," she said, as they continued into what she assumed was the living area.

"Yeah, it is. Lincoln did most of the work."

"Is this your house?" She looked around.

"Naw." He laughed. "I wish."

"Fitzgerald . . . who's out there?" a woman called.

"Hold on, I'll be right there."

"Okay, what's going on?" Yaya asked. "Why am I over here with you and some woman?"

"Where's your stuff?" He frowned.

"What stuff?" She looked at him.

"Your make-up stuff—I told you to bring it."

"It's in the car."

"Why did you leave it in the car?—that's the point of your being here. Why do you think I told you to bring it?" He sighed. "Where are your keys. I'll get it."

"You had me drive all the way over here to do someone's face?"

"Yeah." He rushed out the door. He returned with her two large bags in tow. "Damn, all this is make-up?"

"Uh, yeah, and I have another bag in the trunk," she said. "You better tell me what's going on before I do anything."

"Fine. Come on." He led her down a hallway.

They came to a closed door and he opened it slowly. It was dim inside due to the curtains being closed tightly. Yaya could make out a shadow sitting on what appeared to be a bed. The only light came from a small lamp on a bedside table.

"Hey, I'm coming in. I brought somebody with me."

"Who? Who's with you?" the woman screeched. "You know I don't want to see anybody! Get out. Get out now!"

Yaya stopped in her tracks and turned to leave, but she felt Fitz's hand hold hers. A spark of electricity went up her arm, and her fingers clasped around his. She began breathing harder, and her heart began beating faster. Her mind was thinking of a hundred different things at once. *Why am I here? Who is this woman? What are they about to do to me? What does he want from me?*

Yaya became scared. Not only because she didn't know the answer to any of those questions, but also because she knew that when Fitz's hand touched hers, it sparked something inside of her. Something she had never felt before.

"I'm about to turn the lights on," Fitz said. "We're not leaving."

"Don't turn them on, Fitzgerald," the woman pleaded. "I'm asking you not to."

"It's okay. She's here to help you, that's all," he said, softly. He released Yaya's hand and she saw him walk over to the bed.

The woman turned her back to him. Yaya could hear her crying. She could see the silhouette of Fitz putting his arm around her and comforting her.

Yaya gently put her bags down and walked over to the dimmer switch near the doorway. She slowly turned the lights up just enough so she could see better. She noticed the woman had on a loose-fitting robe and was trembling. Her eyes fell on the nightstand and saw bottles of medication and a book on healing. She closed her eyes and asked God for direction, something she hadn't done in a long time.

Feeling confident, she finally spoke. "Hi, I'm Qianna." She walked closer to the bed.

"Please, go away," the woman told her.

"Nope," Yaya told her.

The woman's head turned toward her. "What did you say?"

"I said, 'Nope.' I'm not going away. Fitz will tell you—I don't like being told what to do."

"That's true; she's just as stubborn as you are, believe me, if not worse." Fitz laughed. "Yaya, this is my aunt, Natalie."

"Nice to meet you." Yaya walked over and was now facing both of them.

The woman hesitated and looked up.

Yaya saw that her face was swollen from what looked like months of crying, and her head was completely bald.

"Yaya, would you believe today is her sixtieth birthday, and she doesn't want to see anyone? We planned a celebration dinner and everything, and she's refusing to even attend."

"I don't want people to see me like this, Fitzgerald, and I'm not in the mood for celebrating. Qianna, if you had gone through everything I've been through these past six months, I guarantee you wouldn't feel like celebrating either."

"That's not true. Fitz, can you get me some towels?"

"Sure. I'll be right back." He quickly left the room.

"I've been through more surgeries and chemotherapy than a little bit. I've been fighting breast cancer for over thirteen years, and I'm tired. What do I have to celebrate?"

Yaya walked over to the windows and began pulling the shades open. Sunshine began flooding into the room.

"What do you have to celebrate?—Life!" Yaya smiled as she grabbed one of her bags. She put her After Effex cape over her clothes and set up the materials she knew she would be working with.

She heard the doorbell ring in the distance. Yaya pulled out her iPod and speakers, finding a nearby plug.

"What is all this? What are you about to do?" Natalie asked.

"Hey," Camille's voice came out of nowhere.

Yaya frowned. "What are you doing here?"

Camille held out Yaya's cell phone. "You left this at the shop. I knew you were going out of town, so I brought it to you."

Surprised by the girl's thoughtfulness, she said, "Thanks. But how did you know where I was?"

"You left the directions on a piece of paper on the counter. I told Monya I would bring it to you."

"Wow! I appreciate that Camille," Yaya told her. "Oh, Natalie, this is Camille."

"Hi," Natalie said, her voice barely above a whisper.

"Hello." Camille smiled at her. "You need anything else?" she asked Yaya.

Yaya thought for a moment. "No, that's it. I wish I had found my brushes, though."

"I have some in my truck you can use."

"No. I use M•A•C brushes. Thanks, anyway."

"I know, those are the only ones I use." Camille laughed. "I don't have all of them, but I have a nice set. I'll be right back."

Yaya was shocked when Camille returned, make-up bag on her shoulder. She watched as she reached inside and pulled out a black zippered bag and passed it to her.

Just as Camille told her—they were the exact brushes she needed.

"These are yours?—these are expensive." Yaya looked at the brushes, each of which cost no less than thirty dollars.

"Yeah, they're mine, and I know how much they cost." Camille laughed. "I've been buying like one or two a week this summer. Like Taryn said—you have to sacrifice to be a master at your craft; I look at it as an investment."

Yaya smiled. "That's the right way of looking at it."

"You can take them with you to D.C. Just be sure to bring them back," Camille told her.

"Really? Thanks a lot. I really appreciate that, Camille. And don't worry, I'll take great care of them."

"Well, it was nice meeting you, Ms. Natalie. Yaya, have a good trip."

"She's nice. Who was that again?" Natalie asked, when Camille was gone.

"She's my new employee," Yaya told her.

"Everything all right in here?" Fitz asked, passing Yaya the towels.

"Yes, everything is fine," Yaya answered. She clicked her iPod on and found the playlist labeled 'Gifted and Talented.'

As Chaka Khan began singing "I'm Every Woman," she began swaying.

"Fitz, you can be excused. We'll call you when we're ready."

Yaya worked tirelessly on Natalie's face as what she called her "I-am-woman, hear-me-roar" songs cheered her on.

She began by giving her an herbal facial.

By the time she finished applying her make-up, Natalie looked like a brand-new woman and was singing along with Gloria Gaynor's "I Will Survive."

"Well . . . all done." Yaya stood back and admired her work.

"Oh, my! I'm scared to look," Natalie said.

"Why? Didn't we just get finished singing that you were beautiful, no matter what they say?" Yaya laughed. "You were beautiful before I even put the make-up on; this is just an enhancement, like rims on a car."

"Uh, I wouldn't call it that."

"I couldn't think of any other analogy. Let me get my mirror for you so you can see."

"Wait," Natalie said, as Yaya passed her the mirror.

"You look fine, trust me. No one would ever know you're turning sixty today."

Natalie began laughing heartily.

Yaya placed the mirror in her hand, and she looked into it.

The laughter stopped, and she touched her face. Tears began to form. Gone was the ashen skin and sunken look of her face. She now looked years younger; her eyes were brighter, and she was glowing.

"What . . . you don't like it?" Yaya began to get nervous. "I can change it."

"No, it's-it's-I . . ."

"What? I'm sorry, Ms. Natalie. Is it too much?" Yaya went and sat beside her and put her arms around her.

"It's beautiful. I've never seen myself like this. No one has ever done this for me before, not even at the television studio," she whispered.

"'Television studio'?" Yaya repeated. Then it dawned on her exactly who this woman was. "Oh my God, you're Natalie Frazier!"

"No, I *was* Natalie Frazier, now I'm Natalie Doles."

"I knew I'd seen you somewhere before."

Yaya recalled how, as a child, she grew up watching this beautiful black woman on the news every evening. Natalie Frazier was her idol.

"I wanted to be you when I grew up!"

"Honey, what you are now, what you just did is better than anything I could have ever done—you have a gift."

There was a knock at the door.

"Uh, it's after five, Yaya, and you said your plane leaves at six-thirty."

"Thanks, Fitz. You can come in now." Yaya began packing her things quickly.

Fitzgerald walked in. They could hear him take a breath when he saw Natalie. "Oh my God, you look beautiful."

"No, she was beautiful before I got here; now she's stunning."

"Yeah, like some stunning rims on a car," Natalie added.

"Huh?"

"Never mind. It's a woman thing, you wouldn't understand. Well, Ms. Natalie, I have a plane to catch. It has certainly been a pleasure this afternoon. And I hope to see you really soon. As a matter of fact, call and set up an appointment for next week because we really need to start doing a facial on you regularly, clear those toxins out of your skin."

Yaya gave her a business card and a hug.

Natalie continued to primp in the mirror. "Shoot! Fitz, we may need to stop and get me a wig on the way to the restaurant."

"I think you've created a monster." He laughed as he carried her bags to the car.

"Good. I've been needing some company in the monster department anyway."

"Thank you so much. Wow! I can't believe what you did to her. She's like a new woman. She's been acting like a zombie since she was released from the hospital last week. Wouldn't get out of bed or anything. How much do I owe you?"

"Nothing." Yaya smiled and opened the trunk so he could put the bags in.

"'Nothing'?—Didn't I tell you earlier about insulting me and my pockets?"

The way he was looking at her made her feel self-conscious. She rubbed the back of her neck. "I wasn't trying to insult your pockets. You just don't owe me anything, that's all. I gotta get outta here or I'm gonna miss my flight."

"Have a safe trip."

They both stood looking at each other for a few moments.

"Oh, wait, I almost forgot!" Yaya reached into the car and grabbed her camera. "I gotta take a picture." She ran back inside.

"She's not gonna let you do that."

Within seconds, she returned, showing him the screen, his aunt posing with the biggest smile he had ever seen.

Chapter 24

"Now, what is this I hear about your not coming to your mother's house?"

"Nothing, Daddy," Paige told her father as he walked through the door. She knew something had to be going on for him to drive all the way over here on a Friday night, rather than hang out and play cards with his buddies.

"Well, it's gotta be something—that's your mama."

She sat down on the sofa, and he sat beside her.

"Daddy, she's letting Aunt Gayle and Celeste stay with her. You know I don't like them, and they don't like me. How could she even let them stay with her?"

"Paige, you know you sound ridiculous. That's her sister, and she's sick. You know your mama is gonna do everything in her power to help out. Now, if that means taking them in for a while, then so be it."

"Then, I won't be going over there until they leave, so be it." Paige laughed.

"So now you want your mother to be caught in the middle? You know your mama don't call me for nothing unless it's bothering her."

"I don't want that at all." Paige began picking at a thread on the arm of the sofa.

Her father was right. He and her mother separated when she was months old, and he still provided for her. After all this time, her mother never asked for anything, but he continued to pay all her bills, saying she was still his wife and he would always take care of her. They had the strangest relationship Paige had ever witnessed, but they were her parents and she loved them. She also knew that they loved each other too. She knew her mother was disappointed when she told her she had nothing to say to her once she found out she had taken in Aunt Gayle and Celeste. Now, knowing that she called her father, Paige knew her mother had been even more upset than she'd thought.

"Well, that's how she feels, and she's felt that way for a long time now. This thing with Celeste and Gayle has gotten out of hand. You all are coming to blows, now? Come on, I thought I raised you better than that."

"You did, it's Celeste that was half-raised. I think you and Mama did a fine job myself; I'm not the crazy one. Think about it, Daddy—they could've gone and stayed with Aunt Connie, or look at that big house Meeko lives in. She would've gladly taken Aunt Gayle and Celeste in and hired a private nurse. I know for a fact she offered to do that and they declined. They moved in with Mama to cause dissension between me and her."

"If that's the case, then their plan worked, because you and your mother are at odds. You told her not to bother coming to Myla's soccer game? Now that wasn't right."

"Okay, I was wrong for that, and I'll call and apologize." Paige nodded. "But I'm not going over there until they're gone for good."

"Don't be like that, Paige." He sighed. "I understand how you're feeling. There have always been some underlying issues with Gayle and Celeste."

"I don't understand why, though, Daddy."

"Well, I may be the cause of some of it."

Paige looked over at her father. "Why? What did you do?"

"Well, back when we were younger, Gayle had a thing for me and I knew it. But I was interested in Jackie, so I became friends with Gayle to get in good with your mama."

"Daddy, you used Aunt Gayle to get with Mama? That ain't right." Paige shook her head.

"I didn't say it was something I was proud of. Well, to keep the peace, your mother and I kinda kept things under wraps for a while, but when Gayle found out, it wasn't pretty at all. She did everything in her power to make our lives miserable. And to this day, Gayle is still guilt-trip-ping your mother about it. She always says your mother took away her one chance at happiness."

The story sounded so familiar, Paige felt like she was living it. In actuality, it was the same situation she found herself in, regarding Quincy and Celeste.

"Then Mama should understand what I'm going through," Paige said. "Besides, Aunt Gayle married Celeste's dad."

"And before she could give birth, he commit-ted suicide, leaving a note saying he wasn't ready to be a father or a husband."

"Wow! That's crazy. I never knew Celeste's dad did that."

"Those two have been sad and depressed all their lives," her father told her. "They want ev-eryone else to be sad and depressed too. Don't let them get their satisfaction by seeing it happen—talk to your mother."

"I'll talk to her, Daddy, but I'm not going over there."

"Well, that's at least a start. What time is Ms. Myla coming home?"

"Camille took her and Jade down to the beach after they finished soccer practice."

"Well, tell her I can't wait until her big game." He stood up and gave her a big hug. "I love you."

"Love you too, Daddy."

Chapter 25

"Oh my God! I think I'm in love! You have got to be the most beautiful woman in the world!"

Yaya cocked her head to the side and rolled her eyes. "You said the same thing to Sophia twenty minutes ago, Diesel, not to mention, you say it every time you see me."

"And I mean it each time I say it, baby. I asked you to marry me a long time ago, and you turned me down." He grabbed her hand, pulled her to him, and kissed her neck.

"You also asked Taryn that same night, along with three other dancers at the party." Yaya tried to push him away.

"But I was only serious about you," he said, looking into her eyes.

If she didn't know any better, she would've thought he was being honest, but she had learned a lot about Diesel over the years. She knew that there was no truth to what he was saying. She had fallen for his game twice and wasn't about to fall for it again.

The name *Diesel* suited him perfectly. He stood six feet, five, and he was big, but sexy. His caramel complexion, dark eyes, long lashes, and inviting smile were enough to have women at his beck and call. And his personality was an added bonus; seduction came naturally to him. People loved to be around Diesel, and Diesel loved people.

"So what are we doing tonight?" she asked.

"Well, I've already made arrangements for each of you to receive a full body massage in your suite once we've finished down here, for starters. I want all of you to be completely relaxed for tonight's festivities," he told them, as they sat in the restaurant of the Marriott, eating brunch.

"And just what will we be doing tonight? And who will be attending?" Yaya asked. "I'm telling you, Diesel—you know I ain't down for any and everything."

"Well, I am," Gabrielle said, sexily.

Yaya ignored her. "I'm serious."

"Calm down. You know I wouldn't even do you like that; you're my girl. Have I ever asked you to do anything out of the ordinary?"

Yaya gave him a knowing look.

"Okay, maybe I didn't phrase that right—Have I ever asked you to do anything to disrespect you and your body?"

She continued to stare. The look on her face didn't change.

"Damn, Yaya! You know what I mean. It ain't that type of party."

Yaya asked again, "So what will we be doing?"

"Don't worry, you'll be doing the one thing I know you're the best at, baby." He leaned over and whispered in her ear, "You'll be making art."

"Wow! I've never seen anything like this in my life," Sophia said as they walked into the building where they were told to be.

The white walls of the corridors seemed to go on forever, and the ceiling was painted pitch-black, with white lights. Bright, bold, eclectic paintings hung on the walls. Techno music pumped loudly, and they could feel the bass through the floor.

"Is this where we're supposed to be?" Gabrielle asked. "I think we're the only people here; I don't see anyone else."

"Yeah. The girl outside said the door at the end of the hallway. Come on." Yaya looked around.

"I don't even see a door," Sophia said.

They walked a little further and, sure enough, came upon a door. Yaya knocked and opened it at the same time.

"Welcome, ladies!" Diesel called out to them.

"Where the hell are we?" Yaya asked. "What is this place?"

"It's The Rouge," Diesel told her.

They entered into a huge room. The walls were covered in mirrors and lights. There was a bar that spanned the entire length of the back wall, and a stage just as large in the front. On one end there was a DJ booth.

"It's a new club that's about to open in a few weeks. No one knows about it yet, except for the people coming tonight, so consider yourselves lucky. Come on, I'll show you to the back, where you can get changed."

Diesel led them behind the stage area and into a large dressing room, where trays of fruit and bottled water awaited them. There was even a large vase of tulips, which he picked up and gave to her.

Yaya smiled. "For me?"

"I know they're your favorite." He reached into the inside pocket of the black linen jacket he wore with his dark jeans, and placed an envelope in her hands.

She placed it into her Coach purse, without even opening it, knowing it held her normal fee, plus an added bonus. Diesel always hooked her up.

"You have about an hour to get changed, and then I can take you all onstage once everyone gets here."

"Diesel, you haven't even told me how you want me to do their faces. I know you have a theme," Yaya told him. "Where are the other dancers?"

"These two are it, and they won't be dancing."

"Oh, hell no! What are we gonna be doing then?" Sophia looked like she was about to walk out.

"Modelling."

"What are they wearing?" Yaya asked, now curious herself.

"Their bodies." He smiled. "Come on, I'll show you."

They followed him out the door and onto the stage. The curtains were closed, but they could hear male voices on the other side. Toward the front of the stage, in the middle, there were two white leather sofas and a nice-size oval table with buckets and brushes.

Yaya walked over and looked at the buckets and saw that it was paint. She realized what it is he wanted her to do. She looked over at Diesel and smiled at him. "You are crazy," she said.

"That shit is gonna be so hot." He nodded, seeing that she understood what he wanted.

"Come on, ladies," she told them. "Let's go get ready."

"I still don't get it." Gabrielle sighed.

"Don't worry," Yaya assured her, "it's gonna be fun."

Diesel left the room, saying he'd be back to get them once the party got into full swing.

They went back into the dressing room, where Yaya changed her clothes. She went into her bag and took out a pair of scissors, removed the hundred-seventy-dollar jeans she wore, and began cutting them.

"What are you doing?" Sophia asked, wide-eyed.

"Getting my costume ready." Yaya laughed.

Satisfied with her creation, she put on what were now short shorts with ravels hanging. She told the girls to undress completely, down to their panties. She was happy to see that they both wore lace thongs. She then oiled both their bodies down.

As she worked, her phone began ringing. She checked and saw that Jason was calling for the hundredth time. He had been calling, upset that she wasn't attending the retreat with him. He even tried to convince her to meet him Sunday morning, which she declined. She was beginning to see more and more that maybe there was some truth to what Monya and Taryn were telling her. She ignored the call and kept working.

Diesel's head popped in the door. "You guys ready?"

Yaya saw his eyes bulge when he saw the half-naked woman standing in the middle of the floor.

"No, she hasn't even started the make-up," Gabrielle said.

"I'm not doing make-up," Yaya said. She checked herself in the mirror. "Diesel, grab that bag and carry it out to the table for me. And I know you got me a drink waiting."

"Apple Martini with a double-shot of Grey Goose already waiting for you, baby." He grabbed the bag she was pointing to.

They walked back onto the stage. The music was on full blast now.

"What song you want?"

"Something slow and seductive to begin with." She winked. She changed into a pair of black pumps and tied her blouse into a midriff shirt.

"Damn! Y'all are sexy as hell. These guys are about to flip the hell out," Diesel told them.

They went out and took their places on the stage. Yaya told each lady to choose a sofa, lie down, and strike a sexy pose. She took a swallow of her drink and nodded to let Diesel know she was ready.

"What's up, fellas? You know we're glad you all decided to come out and hang with us, and since you're here, we want you to eat, drink and be entertained," Diesel said into the microphone.

Someone yelled from the crowd, "That's right, D!"

"We know you got something for us, Diesel. Bring it on!"

"A'ight, a'ight. I wanted to do something unique, so I called up a friend of mine and asked her to come out here and do what she does best. So I present to you, Ms. Yaya and Mystique!"

The lights dimmed, and slowly the curtain opened.

Yaya could hear the opening music of Janet Jackson's "Any Time, Any Place." She opened the can of paint and poured it into a small bowl. She glanced up at the audience and stretched seductively. As she looked out, she saw faces of professional athletes and rappers that she had seen over the years. *Damn! It's some ballers up in here!*

Yaya walked over to Sophia and took each of her arms into her hands, then placed them over her head. "Arch your back," Yaya told her softly. "Now lay back and smile softly."

Sophia looked at her, doing what she was told. "What are you about to do?"

"Paint you." Yaya took a brush, dipped it into the paint, and then placed it on Sophia's body, using soft strokes. The bronze color tinted her skin immediately.

"Daaaaaammmmmmmnnnnn!" Men screamed as Yaya painted.

She began to concentrate on her task at hand, as a techno beat pumped along with Janet's singing. The lighting changed, and a red spotlight was on them.

Yaya took turns, sensually painting each of their bodies. It was a truly artistic experience, and Yaya enjoyed it.

The men seemed to be hypnotized by what she was doing, especially when she lifted breasts and spread their legs to paint.

They are so pitiful. All I'm doing is putting bronze paint on these women, and they are gawking like they've never seen a nipple before.

Camera phones were everywhere, and Gabrielle and Sophia even posed and smiled.

"I've never seen anything like this before," Yaya heard one man say. "What's your name?"

Yaya turned to see one of the country's hottest rappers talking to her. "Qianna."

"That's what's up." He raised his drink to her.

As if they were just now discovering that she could talk, men began walking up to the stage, making comments and asking Yaya and the girl's questions.

They had a blast, being the center of attention, and Yaya was in her element. She couldn't help noticing that the few women in attendance didn't seem pleased with their artistic display.

"Excuse me, Ms. Yaya, how much would you charge to do my lady friend right here for me?" One guy pointed to a lady who was holding on to his arm so tight, it looked like she was made on to it.

Yaya recognized him as a player for the Lakers. She had been to a couple of parties that he had been to. The woman on his arm wasn't the wife he was usually with.

"I didn't say I wanted to do that." The girl turned her nose up at Yaya and then looked at him.

"Fine then." He removed his arm from hers.

Another girl was walking by, and he spoke to her, whispering into her ear.

The girl laughed and nodded her head.

He looked back at Yaya. "Ms. Yaya, how much would you charge me to paint her?"

Yaya looked up from Sophia's legs. "A thousand dollars."

"Done!" He reached into his pocket and pulled out a wad of cash.

"You're serious?" She looked over at the girl he was pointing to, a pretty young woman who looked to be no more than nineteen.

"I don't mind," the girl said, looking eager.

"You can go get changed in the back then."
Yaya pointed.

The first female hissed at the basketball player.
"What the hell do you think you're doing? How
are you going to just push me aside like I'm a
nobody?"

"You are." He laughed. "You ain't nobody
special, besides, I would rather see her painted
than you anyway—she has a better ass."

The woman stormed away in anger, as the
crowd of men laughed.

"You know you were wrong." Yaya shook her
head at the guy.

"I'm sorry, Ms. Yaya, but ol' girl needs to
remember her place. She's up in here acting like
she ain't *paid* to be here." He laughed. "No disrespect to you or your beautiful models up there,
but with you all we know your sole purpose is
entertainment *for* the party. With ol' girl, she's
entertainment for the *after*party, know what I
mean, fellas?"

"True dat, man."

The guys around him laughed.

Yaya turned her attention back to Sophia and
Gabrielle, telling them they could go ahead
and change into their clothes, and mingle with
the guests if they wanted to.

"Uh, can I just wear a robe?" Sophia looked down at her bronze body. "I'm not putting my BCBG dress over this paint. Is this stuff even gonna wash off?"

"Girl, yeah, it'll wash off, that's why I oiled you down first. When you jump in the shower, you'll see." Yaya laughed. "I'm about to grab something to eat right quick."

"Is that girl really gonna get up here?" Gabrielle asked.

Yaya admired her own artistry. This was a wonderful idea, and she was glad Diesel had thought of it.

"She says she is, and he's already paid me." Yaya laughed. "If she doesn't, he's not getting a refund either."

"I know that's right." Sophia laughed.

"Excuse me, can I get a picture with you three?" someone asked.

Yaya looked over at the other girls. "Sure."

After posing for several shots, Yaya excused herself. "I'm about to grab something to eat before I start painting again."

"Yeah, because it looks like she's ready." Gabrielle pointed to the girl peeking from behind the stage.

Yaya walked over to her. "You don't have to do this. It's not a big deal."

"No, I'm cool. I'm just glad I wore cute underwear." The girl laughed.

"Join the club," Yaya told her. "What's your name?"

"Miriam, but they call me Magic. And, no, I'm not a stripper; it's a nickname my mom gave me when I was born."

"Okay, Magic, let me grab something to eat, and we can go ahead and get started, okay?"

"That's cool. Take your time. I won't be going anywhere."

As Yaya was making her plate, Diesel walked up behind her and kissed her neck. "Baby, you know you are the best, right?"

"That's what they all say." She turned around. "I must admit, Diesel, this was a hot idea. Those guys are going crazy. I even got another girl to paint."

"Who?" He stepped back. "I ain't paying for another chick."

"Calm down, boy. I've already been paid."

"By who?"

"Him." Yaya pointed to the ballplayer who had commissioned her to paint Magic. He was standing at the other end of the buffet table, talking.

"I'm not surprised. Hell, he brought a couple of his girls for the guys to enjoy after they leave here."

"What do you mean?—You make him sound like a pimp." Yaya laughed and reached for another shrimp.

"I didn't say that."

Yaya looked over and saw the girl who had declined to be painted earlier, standing with her arms folded. Yaya could see she still had an attitude.

"So, tell me, what does a brother have to do to get with you?" Yaya heard a guy ask as he walked up to the girl.

"Excuse me?" The girl scowled at him. "You don't have enough money to even smell this!"

"Girl, stop trippin'. I wasn't even talking about getting no ass. I was trying to take you out on the serious tip, but now that I see you're a ho, I changed my mind."

The girl's face frowned even harder. "What did you call me?"

"I said you're a ho, your mama was a ho, and chances are, your mama's mama was a ho!" The guy laughed loudly now.

The girl raised the drink she was holding and tossed it into his face.

In a flash, the guy reached over and grabbed the buffet table and flipped it on the girl.

As if in a dream, Yaya stood and watched, unable to move.

The girl screamed, as she crumbled to the floor, her face and body covered in food.

Glass shattered, and people began rushing over to see what had happened. Security came from nowhere, grabbing both the guy and the girl and escorting both of them out of the club.

"Yo, you a'ight?" Diesel asked.

"Huh?" Yaya was still stunned by what had taken place.

"Yaya!"

"Yeah, I'm good."

Yaya could feel someone staring at her, making her uncomfortable. She turned to see Jason's best friend, Travis Thorne, standing with a smug grin on his face.

Chapter 26

"What do you want?—It's late, and Myla's asleep."

"I just called to give you my new information."

"What new information?"

"I moved out."

"What? When?"

"Two days ago."

Paige sat back, stunned at what Marlon had just told her. She couldn't believe it. "So what happened?"

"Nothing major. I just got tired, I guess. I never loved Kasey anyway, you know that."

"What about the baby?"

"What about it? I'm gonna take care of my responsibilities. I don't have to be with her in order to do that; you should know that, of all people."

"And what about your mother?"

"What about her? She has what she wants now—a full-time nurse, a maid, a companion, and a grandchild all in one." He laughed.

"That's not funny, Marlon. Where are you gonna live?"

"I got an apartment."

"That's crazy."

"When is Myla's first game?"

"Saturday after next."

"I know she's excited. When I talked to her the other day, soccer was all she could talk about."

"Yeah, I'm sick of hearing about it myself," Paige told him. It was as if Myla walked, talked, and breathed soccer.

"I'm glad you let her play. You are doing a great job with her, Paige; I know I don't tell you that often enough."

Paige could see where the conversation was headed. "Thanks, Marlon. Look, I'll see you at the game in a couple of weeks. I'm glad you are getting yourself together."

She hung up the phone and flipped the TV on. She didn't even realize she had fallen asleep, until Camille walked through the door.

Camille had been working so hard, that she hardly ever saw her. "Girl, you scared me." Camille laughed, putting her keys on the coffee table.

"You must've been up to no good then," Paige told her. "How's work?"

"Work is wonderful!" Camille smiled. "I love it. I love working with Taryn, and I'm learning so much. It's great!"

"That's good. But, Cam, I'm telling you, August is right around the corner, and you're going back to school. There's no way I'm going to let you just throw away a free college education. You worked hard for that scholarship. Not only that, but Marlon worked hard helping you as well. You don't want to disappoint him."

Camille looked down at the floor. "I know, Paige. Speaking of Marlon . . . he moved out."

"I know. He called and told me." Paige sighed. "Mama has been calling my phone all day leaving crazy messages. She says that we abandoned her and she hates both of us. She says, without her, I'm never going to be anything, like she has anything to do with how far I've come in life so far."

Paige walked over to Camille and hugged her. It was no secret that Lucille was an awful mother. Paige had witnessed and experienced the worst of times with Camille and her mother, but she also knew that Lucille's words still hurt.

The pain in Camille's face when she told Paige about her mother's messages, was obvious.

"Cam, she was drunk. I don't even have to listen to the messages to know that."

"But that's when she's the most honest, Paige
. . . when she's all liquored up." Camille shook
her head.

Paige hated Lucille for the damage she was
still causing in Camille's life. Even though Camille had moved out and moved on with her life,
Lucille continued to menace the girl.

"The sad part is, no matter what I do, how far I
try to get away from her, she still won't just leave
me the hell alone."

"Camille, there's nothing you can do or say to
change your mother or her ways; she's just her.
What you can do is continue to move ahead and
do the right thing and prove her wrong—that's
revenge of the best kind. She can't take away your
success, no matter how hard she tries. You've got
to know that what God has for you is for you, and
your mother and no one else can take that away
from you. Believe me, I know," Paige said with
tears in her eyes. "I don't care what anybody says
or does, you are meant to walk in greatness, no
matter what. Your happiness is ordained!"

"Are you talking to me?" Camille laughed.
"For a minute, it sounded like you were talking
to yourself."

"You know what, Cam, if I wasn't, maybe I
shoulda been." Paige smiled.

"You know, I was gonna mention that to you."
Camille smirked.

"Don't even try it."

"I don't know who was crazier, Quincy for letting you go or Marlon for not holding on to you," Camille said. "You are one in a million."

Paige thought about what Camille said. It was one of the greatest compliments anyone had ever given her, and she realized that she was right. She had been having a pity party of her own, thinking that there was something wrong with her, when it was Marlon's and Quincy's loss. One thing she was determined not to lose was her relationship with her mother.

"What are you doing here?" Aunt Gayle asked, when Paige walked in the following morning.

"I'm here to see my mother. Where is she?"

"She's not here."

Paige raised her eyebrow. "Her car's outside."

"She walked up to the church for a little while," Aunt Gayle answered.

Paige looked over at her aunt and saw just how pathetic she was. She looked much older than her fifty-two years, in her short, faded-red Afro and usual attire of elastic waist pants and an oversize flowered blouse. Paige knew that was exactly how Celeste would look at that age, and she felt sorry for both of them.

"How're you feeling?"

"I'm making it." Aunt Gayle, surprised by the question, looked at Paige.

"You're here alone? Where's Celeste?"

"She ran out to the store to get me some herbal tea. She'll be back in a few minutes."

"Well, I can sit with you until she returns."

"No, I'll be fine." Aunt Gayle began looking nervous. "You go ahead on up to the church. Your mother is there."

"No, its fine, Aunt Gayle. I can stay for a few minutes." Paige sat in a chair.

"Well, I'm a bit tired. I was about to go get in the bed and take a nap." Aunt Gayle stood up so quickly, that she nearly lost her balance.

Paige quickly jumped up and caught her aunt by the arms to prevent her from falling. "Aunt Gayle, what is the matter with you?"

The door opened and Celeste walked inside.

"What are you doing to my mother?"

"She was about to fall. She got up too fast off the chair."

"I told her I was going to be fine and she could go ahead and leave," Aunt Gayle said nervously.

"Yeah, Paige, I'm here now," Celeste said. "You can go and leave us alone."

Paige looked at both of them and wondered what was going on. They were both acting like two teenage girls who had been caught smoking and trying to cover up the scent. She looked at the two pathetic women and decided that finding her mother was more important than being around them.

"Well, take care of yourself, Aunt Gayle."

"I will."

"You want me to call your mother and tell her you're on your way?" Celeste escorted Paige toward the door.

"No, I can just go up there. By the time you talk to her, I'll be there."

"Good-bye," they both said to each other.

Paige got into her car and drove the four blocks to the church. Her mother was making copies in the church office when she arrived.

"Hey, Mama."

"Well, isn't this a nice surprise." Paige's mother gave her a kiss on the cheek.

"I went by the house and Aunt Gayle told me you were here." Paige sat in a nearby empty chair.

"Yes, I had to run up here and run these programs off for Sister Amelia's funeral day after tomorrow."

"Sister Amelia died? Wow! What was she, like a hundred and three?"

"Shut your mouth, Paige Micheals." Her mother laughed. "You know she was only ninety-two."

"Close enough."

"Yes, she lived a full life." Her mother picked up the program and looked at it. "Lived to see her children, grandchildren, and great-grand-children."

"A little while longer and she woulda seen her great-great grandchildren—you know that Aisha is buck wild."

"Shhh . . . be quiet. You know someone may hear you. She was truly blessed, though. I pray the Lord lets me live long enough to experience that."

"He will, Mama." Paige picked up some of the programs and began helping her mother fold them.

"I'm having a hard enough time dealing with you and Myla. I don't know if I can take a third generation."

"What's wrong with me?"

"You're stubborn like your father—Everything has to be your way, and you never want to see things from anyone else's perspective. Your being an only child has something to do with that, too, though."

"I don't try to be difficult, Mama, I swear, but it's like you don't see what Aunt Gayle and Celeste are trying to do."

"They can't do no more than what you allow them to do, Paige. If you know they're trying to annoy you and get under your skin, then don't let them. The madder you get and the harder you fight, the more they win. Look at how you looked at the brunch at Meeko's house—*You* looked like the crazy one."

"Mama, if you knew half the things Celeste was doing—"

"I know what she's doing. I also know you're giving her all the ammunition; all she's doing is pulling the trigger. You gotta learn how to handle things differently, think smart." Her mother tapped on the side of her head. "I know you're brilliant, Paige—I ain't raise no dumb child. You just gotta learn to use it."

"I feel you, Mama. Are you almost done here? I can drive you home."

"Just about. Let me lock this office up, and then we can go back to the house. If you're in a hurry, you can go ahead. The walking does me good."

"Nonsense, Mama."

Paige waited for her mother.

As they got into the car, she told her, "Aunt Gayle and Celeste were acting all crazy."

"What else is new?" Her mother laughed. "Lord knows, they've been getting on my nerves.

I love my sister and all, but I can't take having her complaining about my house much longer. And that Celeste, that girl is so lazy. I don't see how she keeps that job they're always bragging about. She never goes to work, always complaining about a headache— you'd think she was the one on dialysis, rather than Gayle." Her mother sighed.

Paige laughed so hard that her side began to hurt.

They arrived at the house to find a car sitting out front.

"Who is that?" Paige asked.

"Gayle probably got one of her bingo friends over here visiting." Her mother got out the car.

They could hear loud laughing as they walked toward the house.

"Told you it had to be one of her loud friends." Jackie opened the door and stepped inside.

The laughter stopped immediately.

Paige walked behind Jackie to see what had caused her to stop at the doorway. She looked around her mother's living room. Her heart was beating so fast and hard that she thought she was about to fall out. Red and white spots appeared before her eyes, and she kept blinking to make sure she was seeing correctly.

"What the hell are you doing in my house?"

"Jackie! Don't you stand there and disrespect my guests like that," Aunt Gayle told her.

"You need to get outta my house right now!"

"Aunt Jackie, please . . . I told them they could come by and visit for a little while," Celeste said. "It's my fault."

Paige remained quiet. She knew that if she opened her mouth, she may have ended up putting her hands on someone and going to jail.

"I don't give a damn whose fault it is. I'm telling both of you to get out of my house."

"I see your daughter got her ill manners honestly!"

Paige shook her head, trying to step past her mother.

Jackie put her hand up. "It's okay. I got this."

"Ms. Micheals, we didn't mean to cause any trouble."

"The only trouble will be if you don't hurry up and get the hell out of here before I throw both of you out!" Jackie took a step forward.

"Let's go, Ms. Lucille." Kasey stood up, her fat body wobbling.

Paige's eyes fell on her stomach, which now had a slight bulge to it. She honestly couldn't tell if it was fat or the child she was carrying.

"You don't have to leave, Lucille," Aunt Gayle said. "You sit right there. Jackie, let me talk to you in the kitchen for a moment."

"You don't need to talk to me; we don't have anything to talk about—you need to be talking to them, so they can get the hell out of my house!"

"I can't believe you're acting like this. Kasey and Lucille haven't done anything to you. Now, if this is the way you're going to treat the people who come and check on me in my time of need, then maybe we don't need to be staying with you." Aunt Gayle was now standing directly in front of Jackie.

"You're right—you need to get your shit and get the hell out with them!"

Paige could not believe her mother let the word come out of her mouth. Never in her entire life had she heard a curse word, other than *damn* or *hell*, come from those lips.

"What are you saying, Aunt Gayle?" Celeste asked.

"What?—Did I stutter?—Get out, both you *and* your mama!"

Paige put her hands on Jackie's shoulder. "Ma, don't let them upset you. It's not even worth getting your pressure up."

"Sweetie, my pressure is fine. I'm going into my bedroom and take my shoes off. My feet are killing me." Jackie turned and added, "Make sure they get everything out of that guest bedroom and let me know when they're gone."

"We don't wanna be here in this stanky-ass house, no way. Who the hell does she think she is?" Ms. Lucille yelled. "She's right—Get your stuff, Gayle; you can come and stay at our house! The nerve of her . . . How you gonna say you work at the church and kick your own sister out while she sick?—That's a heathen for you!"

Slap!

The hit came so fast, if Paige hadn't seen it with her own eyes, she would've sworn it didn't happen. She looked to her mother and then to Ms. Lucille, who had been knocked back down to the sofa.

"Oh, hell naw! Kasey, call the damn police. She done assaulted me!"

"Get out my house, now! Or I'm gonna call the police! Believe me, there's more where that came from. I got almost seven years of 'whup ass' built up for you. For years, you treated my daughter like dirt, and I didn't say nothing, because it wasn't my place. But now, you're in my house, and you nor your sloppy daughter-in-law is gonna be in here disrespecting her in my house! Get out, get out, I say. Don't make me go straight 'Madea' on y'all up in here—I got a gun, Gayle, you know that; you betta tell them."

Paige didn't know whether to laugh or be scared of her mother's behavior. It was so unreal that it was comical to her. Aunt Gayle and Celeste hightailed it down the hall. Paige could hear her aunt yelling at Celeste to hurry and get the hell out because Jackie had lost her mind,

"You two had better go wait in the car," Paige told Ms. Lucille and Kasey.

They were still standing there, not knowing whether to move or not.

Jackie opened the door as a hint.

They wobbled out together, arm in arm.

Within seconds, Celeste and Aunt Gayle were coming back down the hall, bags in arms, at a record pace.

"I can't believe you're doing this, Jackie! You know I'm sick," Aunt Gayle told her.

"Yeah—sick in the *head*. And so is your daughter—God bless both of you."

"Don't worry, Mama, we can go stay at Meeko's," Celeste said, tears streaming down her face. She looked over at Paige as if she had some support. "I guess you'll get a good laugh out of this one."

Paige laughed. "You damn right about that."

Chapter 27

"Yaya, here are the pictures I downloaded. They all are really nice. I thought Taryn was the best that was out there; now looking at these, I don't know," Camille teased, handing Yaya the envelope.

"I'm flattered, but I will say *T* is the best. She is the one that taught me everything I know," Yaya told her.

"Yeah, I know that, but you took everything she taught you and took it to another level—that's what being the best is all about. You have to be willing to learn and then be smart enough to build upon it."

Yaya looked at her. Camille constantly impressed her and she respected her more and more each time they talked.

"Oh, I placed another Carol's Daughter order this morning. We were running low, and I didn't want us to be out of stock."

"We just did a big order last week. There was a box still in the storage room. Did you put all of that out?" Yaya flipped through the pictures.

"Yeah, I put that out a couple days ago. I've been recommending products to customers, and they've been selling like hot cakes. I'm telling you, we should add the fact that we're a local retailer to the fliers and ads; it'll bring people through the door."

"That's a great idea. Why don't you call over to the print shop and set that up for me?"

"I actually designed a flier myself . . . if you want to check it out and let me know what you think," Camille said, reluctantly.

"I would love to see it. Look, I'm open to any ideas you have about the salon. We're a growing business, and you're a valuable asset to us." Yaya smiled.

"Uh, I don't think so." Taryn walked into Yaya's office. "This is my personal assistant, thank you."

"I've been thinking Camille may be better suited as our full-time receptionist and head buyer." Yaya smiled.

"Are you serious? I would love that!"

"What am I supposed to do for a personal assistant?" Taryn frowned at Yaya.

"She can still do both jobs. Hell, she's been doing both for the past two weeks now that Celeste's ass has been AWOL. Now she'll be getting two checks instead of one."

"Can I, Taryn? Please? I know I can do both."

"I know you can too, Camille. You're going to do great things here. That's why I brought you on board when I did. I knew it was only a matter of time before my so-called partner and best friend saw the light." Taryn smiled. "Now, you think you can go get a sister a smoothie from down the street?"

"Not on company time, I don't think so," Yaya said. "She'd better go answer that phone and take that money from the customers."

"I'll bring you a smoothie back too, Yaya. I know Jetty Punch is your favorite."

"See, that's why I hired her, Taryn. She's beautiful, talented, and brilliant. Reminds me of someone else, huh?" Yaya winked.

"Yeah," Taryn told her. "Me."

"I'll be back in a few minutes."

Taryn sat in the chair in front of Yaya's desk, threw her head back and groaned, "Whhhhh-hyyyyyyyyy?"

"What's wrong, *T*?" Yaya sighed, sensing her best friend's stress.

"I need a drink. What's up with a girls' night at the crib? You down?"

"Why the hell not? I don't have a life after the salon closes anyway," Yaya told her.

"I'll let Monya know. I'm done for the day at six, so I'll go home and get everything ready. Are those your latest pics? Let me see."

Yaya passed the pictures to Taryn.

They looked at them together, talking about the different make-up techniques and styles Yaya used in them. Taryn got a kick out of the pictures from Diesel's party.

"I told you, it was wild!"

"This must be the girl named Magic you were telling me about." Taryn pointed. "She's gorgeous!"

"Yeah, that's her. She lives in ATL. I told her I would try and get her some work. She's definitely not shy, and she has the personality to go a long way."

"Look at Diesel with his fine ass." Taryn laughed. "He is still crazy as hell, I see."

"Yeah, he is. He still hasn't changed. He asked about you. I told him you were in love with Lincoln, though."

"Yeah, right. Not happening."

"Why not?"

"I'll tell you tonight. Who is this woman? She's pretty. I think I know her."

Yaya looked at the picture of Natalie and smiled. "She's a special client of mine."

Taryn looked down at her watch. "I gotta get ready for my next client. Are you hanging these on the wall outside?"

"Yeah. I'm about to come and put them up now." Yaya gathered the pictures and her stapler.

They walked into the main area of the salon. Yaya walked over to what was now known as the "wall of fame."

Camille had collected all of the pictures Taryn, Monya, and Yaya had of all the people they had worked with over the years and made a huge collage.

Yaya took the pictures she had in her hand and added them to the group. She took a step back and looked at the pictures, which included dancers, singers, rappers, actresses, models, men, women, and children from all races, all walks of life.

There was one particular picture that stood out. To Yaya it was her best work ever and meant more than all the faces combined. Natalie Frazier, now Natalie Doles, stared back at her, smiling brightly and confirming something Yaya knew a long time ago, but no one else believed, except for Taryn—this was her calling.

***

"Yaya, you have a call," Camille said, later that afternoon.

Yaya had just completed a facial and was ready to leave for the day. "Hello," she said, tiredly into the phone.

"Hey, Yaya. It's Celeste. I'm surprised that wench let me talk to you."

Yaya ignored Celeste's comment. "What do you want, Celeste? I'm tired and I'm trying to get outta here."

"Oh, okay. I was just calling to see if I can come and get my check because—"

"What check?—You don't have a check, Celeste."

"What do you mean, I don't have a check?"

"Celeste, a check is something you get when you come to work. You haven't been working, so you don't get paid."

"But, Yaya, you know my mother's sick, and then we had to move a little ways out. I don't have a car, so I can't really get there like I want to. It's not like I don't want to get there."

"None of that is my problem, Celeste. I'm sorry."

"Well, can you loan or give me some money like you did before? I don't have—"

"No, Celeste, I'm sorry." Yaya glanced up and saw Camille trying to act like she wasn't listening. "I've gotta go."

"Wait, Yaya . . ."

"What?"

Before Taryn could hear what Celeste was saying, she took the phone out of Yaya's hands.

"Celeste, this is Taryn. Look, listen to me, honey—you're fired. So unless you're calling up here to schedule an appointment, then don't call back— Good-bye."

"*T*, that was cold," Yaya told her.

Monya was tickled to death.

Taryn put the phone down and shook her head. "That girl has issues."

"You don't have to tell me," Camille said.

Yaya was having more fun than she'd had in a long time. She, Monya and Taryn had polished off two large pizzas, a bag of chips, and two bottles of Muscadet wine.

"Now can we get to the point of evening?" she asked.

Monya reached into the bowl and grabbed a handful of chips. "What's that?"

"Well, it seems that my girl here is having Lincoln issues."

"Really? I thought things were going well for you two. Do tell."

"I thought things were going well for us too. You know we've been out a couple of times, had drinks, hung out and played pool. I just assumed things were moving along nicely."

"And they aren't?" Yaya took another sip of wine.

"Apparently not."

Monya shrugged. "He just picked you up the other day and you went to dinner."

"True." Taryn sighed.

Yaya could see the disgusted look on her friend's face. She knew that something had happened.

"We go to dinner and he tells me that I've become one of his closest friends and how much I mean to him. He says that he can talk to me about anything and how he's tired of living his life the way he's been living. He knows that it's time for him to make some serious changes."

"What did he mean by that?"

"Well, it turns out that I'm not the only one Lincoln has been hanging out with."

"Oh, no."

"Yep. He's been seeing several women, and he's also been sleeping with them too. At this point he even has a couple of women stalking him. His cell phone was ringing so much that he wound up just cutting it off so we could talk."

"Wow! Did you sleep with him?" Yaya asked.

"Girl, no. That's the thing. All the times we've been out, he's never tried to make a move on me. It's a good thing too, because you two know me—he coulda got it, with his fine ass."

"Yeah, he is fine, *T*," Monya agreed. "So where do you fit in all of this?"

"He did say he was ready to change, and he knows what he wants," Yaya told her; "that has to mean that he wants to settle down with you."

"I was hoping that's where he was going, but instead, he tells me how I mean too much to him to get involved with now. I'm the only female he can talk to without their being any sexual tension between us. He cares about me too much to be in a relationship with me."

"Oh no, not again!" Yaya groaned.

"*T*, I don't believe this!"

"I'm telling you," Taryn told both of them, "it's a curse!"

"No. It's because you ain't make a move on him, Ms. Take-Your-Time-And-Get-To-Know-Him. Once they know you too much, it's over. I'm telling you, you shoulda told him from the jump you were feeling him." Yaya couldn't help laughing.

Lincoln was the hundredth guy to tell Taryn that he liked her too much as a friend to date her. It was as if she was indeed "man's best friend," in the literal sense. From high school, Taryn had always developed a special bond with guys she liked. They always ended up liking her as a friend, rather than a girlfriend.

"I guess I should be glad, though. From what I gathered, Lincoln has no qualms about who he dicks down. You should hear the stories he told me. Maybe I should be happy I'm not one of his conquests." Taryn poured herself another glass of wine.

"His brother is probably the same way," Yaya said. "Fine or not, that's why I won't get with him."

Monya and Taryn looked over at her.

"What?"

Monya smiled. "So you admit you've thought about Fitz, huh?"

Taryn snapped her fingers. "I knew you liked him."

"No. I said he was *fine*; there's a difference."

"I don't care what you say—you and Fitz are made for each other. I can see it when you look at each other." Taryn stared at her.

"*T*, I could never get with him—he's not my type at all; he's short and light-skinned—let's not mention the dreads, the car, the *kid*!"

"We'll see, Yaya. Fitzgerald Webster is your soul mate; time will tell."

Yaya shook her head in an effort to stop Taryn from talking about it any further, and to rid herself of the image of Fitz's handsome face from her head.

***

The next morning, just as she pulled into the parking lot of the salon and stepped out of her car, Yaya felt someone pulling on her arm.

"I need to talk to you!"

"Jason, what the hell is wrong with you?" She snatched her arm away, realizing who it was.

"Why the hell haven't you been returning any of my calls? And where the hell were you last night? I waited at your house until after two this morning, and you still hadn't come home."

Yaya pulled the strap of her purse over her shoulder and looked at Jason like he had lost his mind.

She walked away without answering and entered the salon. "Morning, everybody."

Jason was still on her heels as she continued to her office. "Don't play with me, Yaya. You owe me an explanation."

"I don't owe you anything, Jason. And you'd better get the hell outta here. How dare you come to my business and embarrass me like this?"

"I haven't embarrassed you . . . yet. I can't believe you carried your ass to D.C. to do a damn freak party with Diesel instead of going with me to the retreat. Do you know how important last weekend was to me? To us?"

"No, Jason, I don't, because there is no more *us*. What the hell are you thinking?—That I'm a damn convenience woman? You don't just call me when you wanna call me and think I'm supposed to jump—my life doesn't revolve around you."

"Then, that's the damn problem. If you're trying to be my wife, like you say you are, then it *should* revolve around me. I'm supposed to be so damn important to you, remember?"

Yaya brushed past him. Thinking he would be too afraid to embarrass himself in front of everyone, she walked back into the main area. She knew people were talking about them.

"Come on, Jason, just leave, okay? We can talk about this later," she said, assuredly.

The door opened, and Fitz walked in, rolling in a dolly full of boxes. "What's up?" he asked, winking at Yaya.

She couldn't help smiling back at him. In an instant she forgot about Jason standing near her.

"Who the fuck is that?" Jason raised his voice.

Fitz stopped dead in his tracks and turned around.

"Jason, you need to leave now," Yaya told him.

"I'm not leaving until you talk to me." Jason looked around and saw he had a full audience. "Ha! Travis told me all about the little freak party you did last weekend—you dancing and painting hookers, and shit—he's got pictures too."

Yaya's face got hot, and she could feel her anger rising. "Jason, leave."

"I see now why you opened this little salon in the hood—you ain't nothing but a common whore your damn self. The way this nigga is looking at you, he's probably boning your ass for a small fee."

The tears Yaya had been fighting rolled down her cheek.

"Jason, that's enough," she could hear Monya saying. "Get out."

"What's up, Mr. Delivery Guy?—You gotta pay for yours or you getting it for free, like I am?"

Fitzgerald hit Jason so hard that it knocked him against the wall, causing the glass shelves to shatter before they hit the floor.

Panic gripped Yaya's heart when she saw the fear in Jason's eyes as Fitz walked over and yanked him up. "Fitz, no!" she yelled, thinking Fitz was about to kill her ex-boyfriend with his bare hands.

Instead, Fitz held Jason by the collar and tossed him out the door.

Yaya ran back into her office and locked the door behind her. She was struggling to breathe.

Moments later, there was a knock.

"Yaya, are you okay?" Camille called out.

In the chaos of what had just taken place, Yaya didn't even see her. "I'm okay. I need to be alone for a while." She sat down and cried harder than she ever had. She couldn't believe Jason had said the things that he did. She was so hurt that she didn't know what to do.

There was another knock at the door.

"I just need to be alone, please."

"I just want to make sure you're okay," Fitz called out to her. "Open the door."

Yaya tried to wipe her face to stop the tears from falling, but they wouldn't. As soon as she opened the door and saw him standing there, she fell into his arms.

"It's all right. He's gone."

She buried her face into his shoulder and allowed him to comfort her.

"I didn't do those things he said I did, I swear. It wasn't a freak party. I'm not like that."

"Don't worry about him. He's not even worth worrying about."

"I can't believe he said that. I loved him, and I thought he loved me. I wanted to marry him and spend my life with him," she cried. "Now what am I gonna do?"

Fitz put his hand under her chin and pulled her head up.

He looked right into her eyes. "Find someone worthy of your love instead. He didn't even deserve to have it." He held her against his strong body once again.

Yaya squeezed her arms around him, thinking if she let go, she would fall.

Taryn's words echoed in her ear as they held each other—*"Fitzgerald Webster is your soul mate, time will reveal."*

Epilogue

"Whoooooo! Come on, Myla! Come on, Jade!" Paige cheered as her daughter's team ran onto the field. She was just as excited as the kids were, wearing her "Proud Mom of #44" T-shirt she had made. She smiled at Nina, who wore her own "Proud Mom of #54" T-shirt.

The crowd cheered. "Let's go, Wildcats!"

Paige looked around and spotted her mother and father, along with Mr. Vernon and Camille's dad, walking toward them. She ran over and gave each of them a hug.

"Wow! Myla and Jade have an entire cheering section." Her father laughed as he spoke to the rest of the clan, which included Camille, Meeko, Stanley, Isaiah, Aunt Connie, and even Titus.

Paige had to give it to him. He was one determined brother. She wished her best friend would wise up and see what a great guy he was and how much he was in love with her.

Myla scored again, and she jumped and screamed.

The game was won, and she hugged him tight.

He looked at her and kissed her tenderly. He knew everyone was watching them, including Marlon, but he didn't care. This time, he was never letting her go.

Camille walked inside the salon. "Lincoln! Where are you?"

There was no answer.

He must've had to run out for a second. She walked past the large empty box that used to house the new princess chair he was installing. She went into Yaya's office and began searching for the contract. It was nowhere to be found.

Just as she was about to call and let her know, she spotted a piece of paper lying on the floor. She leaned down to pick it up and then heard voices.

"Why the hell are you following me around? What the hell do you want from me?" She heard Lincoln say.

"I want you to act like you know me, for starters. You can't just think that this is over, I'm telling you right now," a woman replied.

Camille remained behind the desk, listening.

"It was never anything to begin with. Okay, we kicked it, and I hit it—so what? You act like we were together or something."

"You act like we *weren't* together," the female snapped.

"Look, I don't even know why you're trying to play yourself out like this. I don't even know you, and it's obvious you don't know me—you're straight bananas, chick!"

"You know me well enough to screw me a while back when we left Ochie's. Don't even try to fake like you don't remember. You told me I gave the best head ever while I was going down on you in your van. You weren't that drunk."

"That doesn't say much about you, now does it? Look, if we did do anything, I can guarantee you two things—one, I used a condom because I always do, and two, it didn't mean anything to me. And if you thought otherwise, I'm sorry. So if you think that harassing the hell outta me is gonna get me to believe this bullshit, you're crazy."

"You don't have to believe me, Lincoln. The paternity suit I plan on hitting you with will be proof enough. I heard you talking to Jarrod next door about how you've decided to change and you're thinking really hard about getting with that bitch Taryn, because now you see how much she means to you. Ha! Well, guess what—when she finds out I'm carrying your seed, she ain't gonna have nothing to do with you. And I, for one, am glad, not that it matters anyway. Actually, the only thing that matters is the fact that you're gonna take care of me, and you're taking care of this baby—I mean that."

"Girl, you'd better stop playing with me." Lincoln laughed.

"You think this is a joke? But don't worry, I'm sure it'll be correct on those checks you'll be stroking out to me every month for the next eighteen years. Go ahead and laugh now because, when push comes to shove, I'm taking you down and everyone down with you."

Camille peeked above the desk to see who Lincoln was talking to. She looked up just in time to see the familiar girl storm off. She was so nervous that she almost peed on herself. *Lincoln got this chick pregnant? There's no way! Taryn is going to kill her and him!*

She knew for a fact that withdrawing from school was the best thing for her. Seeing all this unfold right before her eyes, she had no doubt her life at the salon was about to get interesting.